Beautifully Explosive

Candied Crush #11

Charity Parkerson

I0550662

Copyright

The scanning, uploading, and distributing of this book via the internet or via any other means without the permission of the copyright owner is illegal and punishable by law. Criminal copyright infringement, including infringement without monetary gain, is investigated by the FBI and is punishable by up to 5 years in federal prison and a fine of $250,000. Please purchase only authorized electronic editions and do not participate in or encourage electronic piracy of copyrighted materials. Brief passages may be quoted for review purposes if credit is given to the copyright holder. Your support of the author's rights is appreciated. Any resemblances to person(s) living or dead, is completely coincidental. All items contained within this novel are products of the author's imagination.

—Warning: This book is intended for readers over the age of 18.

Introduction

Kit is a little damaged. Matthew is a lot crazy.

Together, they're an explosion waiting to happen.

What would you do if your biggest celebrity crush walked into your life? Matthew has been living this hypothetical question for the past year. There's no other man on the planet that has been a bigger part of Matthew's alone time than Kit Youngblood. Kit is an actor and has posed nude for several adult magazines. Matthew would kill to have one night with Kit. Unfortunately, Kit is nowhere near as easy to catch as Matthew hopes.

Kit doesn't want anyone. It isn't personal. Kit came from a nightmarish background to carve a place for himself in the world. That doesn't mean he's well-adjusted. He's merely surviving the best he can. Matthew is the only person who's made Kit consider taking a chance on a relationship. He just needs a little push to get him moving.

Two men with a boatload of issues and secrets will face off in a battle of the hearts. Only time will tell which of their pasts will break them first. Or just maybe they're exactly what the other needs.

Chapter One

Sometimes, the only comfort Kit found was in a cup of green tea and a book. Even though it was Friday night and slammed, The Back Porch—one of L.A.'s best-kept coffeehouse secrets—was the only place Kit wanted to be. With his book in hand and a cup of steaming tea at his elbow, the noise of the shop disappeared. The hip crowd surrounding him had been replaced by Carlos and Ferdinand as they confessed their love. Romance novels always made Kit's skin tingle, even though it was all bullshit. Spies. Assassins. War heroes. Hell, astronauts. Kit could suspend reality for all the farfetched characters. Real life was different. Kit couldn't halt reality here. There were no men like Carlos or Ferdinand. They were all the antagonist, Enrique, in real life, sending dick pics and saying, "You know you want some of this." Reality sucked.

A shadow fell over the table.

Kit didn't bother looking up from his book. "No."

Another Enrique skittered away.

Kit rolled his eyes. Men were all the same. He turned the page in his book. The sound of sexy laughter penetrated his thoughts. It was a husky rumble—like it would feel good against the shell of his ear. Kit would know that laugh anywhere. He automatically pressed his hand to his stomach as his chin shot up. Sitting diagonally from Kit, within his perfect line of view, was Matthew. Kit couldn't believe it. Since they met a year ago, Kit swore he had gone his entire life without seeing the guy, and now he saw him everywhere. Kit would know if he had seen him before that first meeting. There were men, and then there was Matthew Ross. Sometimes, all Kit had to do was look at Matthew and his day improved. It wasn't that Matthew was sexy. He was, but it wasn't only that. Matthew was the entire package. Smart, funny, and charming. People flocked to him, which was good, since he was a personal trainer and yoga instructor at Kit's gym. His classes were always packed. Everyone was there for Matthew. He single-handedly sold out the gym's water bottles every day when he worked. Matthew made people thirsty as hell. Kit was no exception.

For the past year, Kit had been going to lunch with Matthew at least twice a week. They weren't dating, but—sometimes—it felt like they were. Kit liked that people thought they were a couple everywhere they went. Everyone's misconceptions made him feel less like himself. That was a good thing. As always, when Matthew was around, Kit couldn't look away. Every inch of his exposed skin, except his face, was covered in tattoos. His sleek body looked like it belonged to a yoga instructor. He fascinated Kit, and no one held Kit's attention for long. Matthew was the exception to a lot of rules.

Unfortunately, there was no ignoring that Matthew wasn't alone tonight. Kit's gaze shifted to the man sitting across from Matthew. With his back to Kit, Kit couldn't make out much beyond the fact that he had wide shoulders. The way Matthew smiled—like he couldn't wait to peel away the guy's clothes—had Kit's stomach muscles drawing up tight. Dread had his throat swelling. He had known it was unlikely Matthew went home alone every night. This was the first time Kit had ever witnessed Matthew spending time with anyone else. It hurt.

Matthew turned his head. Their gazes collided. For a moment, Kit stared into Matthew's hazel eyes, and then it hit him. He was jealous.

Kit looked away. He placed his bookmark inside the book and dug some money from his wallet. Kit left his server a twenty-dollar tip since he had held the guy's table hostage for over an hour. With nothing left to distract him, Kit slid from the booth and headed for the door. He was careful not to meet anyone's stare, especially Matthew's. Kit had nothing to offer. Sometimes, he had to remind himself of that when it came to Matthew. But they were friends, so that meant he had to let Matthew be happy with someone else. That knowledge didn't stop Kit from feeling like someone stood on his chest, crushing the air from his lungs.

As he slipped behind the wheel of his Lincoln Navigator, his phone chimed. Kit checked the face.

Matthew: *Come back inside. You can't walk away like you didn't see me.*

For a long moment, Kit considered not answering. In the end, he couldn't be that petty over something Matthew hadn't done wrong. They weren't dating. Matthew didn't owe Kit a thing. He was free to date whomever he wanted. Fuck.

Kit: *I'm working on a migraine, so I'm headed to bed. Enjoy your date. We'll talk soon. XOXO.*

For good measure, Kit turned off his phone. There was no one who would call him in an emergency. He lived with the only couple who cared if Kit lived or died. Over a year ago, Kit's best friend Lucky had gotten married and pretty much dropped Kit. Kit's other friend, Zep, was more like a father figure than anything and that was where Kit lived, so he wouldn't need to call. There was no real family, as far as Kit was concerned. He could turn off his phone without an ounce of regret. No one cared about him or needed him. Kit could disappear right now. No one would look for him. Sometimes, he thought he might do just that one day. He didn't owe this town or anyone in it a goddamned thing. Kit was free.

*

Two years ago, Matthew had been at the darkest point in his life. While on a drug and alcohol self-medicating bender, Matthew had opened a magazine and set eyes on an angel. He had

11

memorized every line. Lusted after every inch of nude skin. Most of all, he had been saved by an unexpected obsession. Then one day, completely out of the blue, that obsession had walked into Matthew's work. At first, he hadn't believed his eyes. Since he had been known to suffer PTSD-induced hallucinations, Matthew hadn't thought Kit was real. Then he had heard Kit speak, and Matthew had nearly hyperventilated.

Matthew had taken a breath, forced his feet to move at a tempered pace, and closed the distance between them. There had been zero chance he would pass up the opportunity to meet Kit, even if he looked like a fool. Their gazes had met, Matthew swore angels had sung, and Matthew hadn't stopped trying to get in Kit's pants since. So far, he hadn't even convinced Kit to hold his hand.

Now, a year later, Matthew was at a new level of desperation to win Kit. He couldn't seem to stop the insanity. Matthew didn't think he was wrong for his obsession, though. He imagined anyone would react the same. Matthew had been given the opportunity to be close to his biggest celebrity crush and he would not stop until Kit either gave in or... he didn't know. He might not ever give up, even if Kit took out a restraining order. Matthew was too far gone already.

Tonight was a good example. The guy sitting across from him at The Back Porch had been asking Matthew to have coffee with him for six months. Matthew had blown him off until tonight. The only reason they were together now was because of Kit. Matthew had known Kit was here. This was a new low. Matthew wanted to make Kit jealous. He had purposely sat in Kit's line of sight. Unfortunately, Kit had been lost in a book, forcing Matthew to talk and laugh louder until he looked like a crazy person. Until their gazes had collided, that is. That moment made Matthew's every desperate move worthwhile.

He hoped Kit's leaving meant he had accomplished his goal. Matthew needed Kit to stop seeing him as only a friend. Sometimes, Matthew caught a hint of interest in Kit's eyes. Matthew had to fan those flames. He had to do this. He had to have this. Matthew couldn't live with any other outcome. Kit had to be his.

He had immediately texted Kit once Kit left the coffee shop. Now, after three unanswered texts in a row, Matthew was torn between giddy and terrified. He might have gone too far. His foot bounced beneath the table. Jeremy droned on and on about the quality of coffee beans in various brews offered by the shop. Matthew lost the battle against himself. He checked his phone again. Still no response.

"I'm sorry," Matthew said, cutting into Jeremy's explanation on how to make cold brew at home. "My mom just texted me that she fell in the shower. I need to go." He slid from the booth, trying to look like the panicked son.

Jeremy's face screwed up in concern. "Oh no. Would you like me to go with you? I could drive."

Matthew dug some money from his wallet. "No. It's fine. Please stay and have another cup on me." He set the money on the table. "Again, I'm so sorry." Matthew quickly bent and kissed Jeremy's cheek, because he was an asshole like that. He raced from the coffeehouse before Jeremy could try stopping him again. It was possible he had ruined his shot with Kit. He had to find out if his plan had worked or fucked him. Matthew knew things could go either way. Kit was a firecracker. He might do anything once his temper was lit.

The second tricky thing about being in love with Kit was that Kit lived with Matthew's boss, Frost. Frost's husband Zep was like a father to Kit, and Kit helped out a lot with the couple's kids. While the living situation gave Matthew another avenue to see Kit more often, it presented a potential problem that could end in Matthew getting fired. While Matthew didn't need the money he made from teaching yoga at Fitness Titan, he needed the peace he received from teaching others how to become more aware of their inner selves.

At Frost and Zep's place, Matthew parked down the street. He stuck to the shadows as he made his way through the yards of million-dollar homes until he could scale the fence surrounding Frost's house. Frost had security cameras. Matthew had subtly changed their directions months ago, so he could chart a path to Kit's bedroom balcony without being seen. He skirted the pool and scaled the tree before leaping onto Kit's balcony. There was a soft light on inside the room—like only the bedside lamp was lit. Matthew knocked on the French doors.

A silhouette moved around inside.

Matthew's stomach muscles clenched in anticipation. He knocked again.

The shadow moved closer. After a moment, the door flew open and Matthew found himself staring down the barrel of a gun. In one swift motion, Matthew disarmed Kit.

"Hi, beautiful. You haven't been answering my texts," Matthew said, handing the handgun back to Kit with the clip out.

Kit didn't look the least bit ruffled. He turned away and set the gun and clip on a table near the door. "I didn't want to disturb your date."

Matthew followed Kit into the room while studying his tone for any hint of jealousy. "I wouldn't have been texting you if you were disturbing me." His voice nearly cracked as he studied Kit's outfit. Kit had on a tiny silk robe and nothing else. It barely covered the assets Matthew had memorized from magazines. Matthew's mouth watered. His palms itched. He had never wanted to touch someone so badly in his life.

"You're supposed to pay attention to your date on a date."

The way Kit kept saying *date* had Matthew looking at him closer. "Are you jealous?"

Kit turned and met Matthew's gaze. He smirked and held his arms out. "Look at me. I don't get jealous. Any man who doesn't want me is dumb as hell. Why would I want a stupid man?"

That one confused the hell out of Matthew. Was Kit saying he thought Matthew didn't want him? Or was he saying Matthew was stupid? Maybe Matthew was dumb as hell because his plan had definitely backfired somehow. He crossed his arms over his chest and tried working it out in his head. Matthew stared at Kit in silence, trying to decide how to respond.

He chose to change tactics and use the moment to his advantage. "You should let me take you to dinner tomorrow night. Not as friends. As a real date, since I'm not the least bit stupid."

"Are you sure about that?"

Matthew's gaze slid down Kit's body. He jerked his stare back to Kit's face. "Yes. No. I don't know. Go on a date with me."

Kit blew out a sigh. "Fine." He headed for the bed.

Matthew fought the urge to jump up and down like an idiot. "You won't regret it."

"I doubt that," Kit said, crawling beneath the covers. "I've been on a thousand actual dates with you over the past year, and you still went out with someone else tonight. So, thus far, I'm not impressed."

Matthew's jaw dropped. Literally. He had never been more shocked in his life. Kit thought they had been dating for the past year while

Matthew thought he had been firmly in the friend zone. He had nothing. A warmth started in his chest and spread. Kit Youngblood thought they had been dating for the past year. A smile tugged at Matthew's lips. He couldn't believe it. For an entire year, he could have been touching Kit. His smile slipped away.

"Wait." Matthew closed the French doors and stamped across the room. "We haven't as much as kissed in the last year. That's not dating. That's friend zone bullshit."

Kit picked up his book, as if barely listening. "How's that my fault?"

Matthew's jaw dropped again. For real, he hadn't known jaws literally dropped when people were surprised before tonight. It had never happened to him before. He had always thought it was a figure of speech. Nope. Kit had managed twice tonight to pull that reaction from Matthew. He could have been kissing Kit fucking Youngblood for the past year. Kit was right. He was stupid. Well, Matthew might be stupid, but he wasn't an idiot. He learned from his mistakes.

With pure determination and hunger in his heart, Matthew closed the final space between them, plucked Kit's book out of his hand, and went in for a kiss.

Kit punched him in the nuts.

Matthew dropped.

With his forehead pressed to the edge of the bed and clutching himself, he sought answers for how he ended up here. "What the hell?"

Kit pried his book from Matthew's hand. "Cheats don't get kisses."

Matthew gasped for air. "So." He panted, trying to catch his breath. "Just to be clear." Matthew wasn't going to make it. Kit had one hell of a punch. "We're dating exclusively, right?"

Kit turned the page in his book. "That's right."

Matthew sprawled out across the floor. "Totally worth it, then."

If he wasn't mistaken, Kit's book hid a smile. Damn. Matthew was batting so far out of his league, he had no idea how he had ended up here. He wouldn't give Kit a reason to call him a cheat again. In fact, Matthew planned to make Kit the happiest man on earth. Once he caught his breath, that is.

Chapter Two

In the year since they had been friends, Kit hadn't been to Matthew's house. With Kit living with Zep and then Zep and Frost, and their houses being five minutes from Matthew's work, they somehow always managed to avoid the topic of where Matthew lived.

Now, with Matthew's address typed into his phone and following Google's directions, Kit had so many questions that he didn't know where to start. Matthew had offered to cook tonight. Kit imagined that was slang for getting Kit into bed. Even though Kit had no intention of doing that, he had still dressed as extra as possible, because that was just who he was. Makeup and pretty clothes were his shields. He wondered now if Matthew's tattoos were his, because Matthew lived two blocks from Kit and his house was twice the size of his boss's. As Kit stood in the driveway of a house that had to cost three million, easy, he wondered how men with money always found him. Kit was never looking.

A woman in the yard next door stared at him as she worked on her garden. Even from a distance, he could feel her disapproval. Kit gave her a tiny finger wave and pranced to the door with a lot of hip sway, working it every step. He lived for pissing off judgmental people. They had no clue what he had survived to come out this fabulous. He refused to tone down his shine for the asshole masses.

When Matthew answered the door, Kit forgot about the neighbor. Matthew wasn't wearing a shirt. His nipples were pierced. Kit's gaze slid down

Matthew's body. He was one giant tattoo. Fuck. He was beautiful.

"Am I early or..."

"Only by a minute or so." Matthew took his hand and dragged him inside. "I just spilled our dinner all over myself. We may be ordering in." Matthew winced. "Sorry."

Kit waved away his apology. "The last time I cooked, a man died. You're fine. We'll figure it out."

A smile snapped to Matthew's lips at Kit's claim. "You're a nut."

He had no idea.

"I can't believe you live so close and in this house. What the hell, Matthew?"

Matthew shrugged. "Would you like a tour?"

"Of course." Kit linked his arm through

Matthew's because he liked touching all the inked skin. As Matthew led him upstairs and pointed out various rooms, Kit puzzled over the complexities of life. Kit did not like to be touched, and he didn't touch other people. Matthew was one of the very few exceptions. Zep and Lucky were allowed to touch him because they were his chosen family. Lucky was his friend, but he felt more like a brother. Zep acted and felt like Kit's dad. Frost occasionally touched his arm or kissed his cheek. Kit never flinched away, but Frost was kind of like a stepdad. The twins were babies. They were harmless. He loved holding them. But he didn't understand why Matthew didn't bother him.

Kit glanced his way. Matthew didn't feel like a brother or a father. He sure as hell wasn't a child. Yet, somehow, Matthew wasn't like everyone else.

Kit wanted Matthew to touch him. He didn't understand.

Matthew led him back downstairs. Kit spotted a pool through the French doors in the formal living room. His curiosity skyrocketed by the second. There was definitely something Matthew hadn't told him. They passed an indoor gym, which seemed crazy since Matthew worked at a gym. Finally, they came to an enormous bedroom. The already high bed sat on a raised area that looked custom made for the massive cherry wood piece. Everything about the house screamed money, character, and taste. Just like Matthew, it was a work of art. Also, just like Matthew, Kit wanted to know more. Matthew had his attention, and it had nothing to do with the money Matthew obviously hid. Matthew had layers. Kit wanted to peel them away.

Honestly, he couldn't get enough.

*

Matthew couldn't stop watching Kit's every reaction. They were so close to his bed now. All it would take was some persuasion. Years of longing and desire fed Matthew's inner darkness. He felt like he stalked Kit, waiting for his moment. In fact, his hands lifted, as if they couldn't wait another second to touch Kit.

Then Kit turned and leaned back against the doorframe, stopping Matthew from touching him the way he wanted. He held Matthew's stare. "So, tell me, how does a yoga instructor afford this house?"

Matthew stepped closer, crowding Kit's space. "I'll tell you as soon as you tell me why a man who's been in several movies and magazines doesn't live on his own?"

Kit's hands landed on Matthew's sides, forcing Matthew to temper his breathing. He couldn't focus on anything beyond the heat of Kit's hands. Kit lightly stroked.

Matthew leaned closer, losing the threads of the conversation. He wanted Kit so badly, it hurt. This was the first time that dream didn't feel out of his reach.

Kit didn't look away. He looked like he was waiting for Matthew to make the first move. His lids lowered as Matthew dipped his head.

The doorbell rang, freezing Matthew in place.

"You have to be fucking kidding me."

He wanted to throw a giant temper tantrum. Matthew wanted to cry. They had been so close to kissing. Matthew was certain of it. He might have stamped a little harder than necessary on his way to the door. His temper spiked when he found Cindy, the HOA president, on his doorstep. She was the nosiest and worst person on the planet. There was nothing he wanted to be doing less than dealing with her right now.

"Hey, Cindy."

A fake smile stretched Cindy's lips. "Hi, Matthew. We noticed you have a guest."

Matthew's smile turned brittle. He wished he wore a shirt. Matthew had lived here for several years now, and he still hadn't figured out who "we" was. "Well, yeah. It's my house. Sometimes I get visitors."

"Oh, of course. You're completely allowed to have whoever you want in your house. That's not the issue. You're a really great guy and we're super proud to have the grandson of a war hero among us."

Jesus fucking Christ. "Thank you."

"We're just a little concerned about the number of homosexuals that are invading us."

Matthew's eyebrows tried crawling toward his hairline.

Cindy wasn't finished. "This is a conservative neighborhood. Everyone has kids here."

"You might be a conservative, but that doesn't make the neighborhood..." Matthew's gaze slid to where Kit stood out of sight of the open doorway. Kit had pulled his shirt higher and tied it beneath his sternum, showing off his flawless stomach, which begged for someone to bite it. By someone, Matthew meant him.

Cindy was still talking about bible verses and

corrupting children. Matthew couldn't focus on anything other than Kit stripping off his pants. He wore a red lace thong. Matthew's body stirred. Before he knew what would happen, Kit skipped his way and launched himself into Matthew's arms. Matthew's hands automatically cupped Kit's bare ass cheeks as Kit's legs wrapped around his waist.

"Come on, Daddy. I'm getting cold. How can you neglect me to play with a girl?"

Even though Matthew grasped that Kit was fucking with the homophobic bitch on his doorstep, his mind wasn't strong enough to handle Kit's half naked body against his. He couldn't pretend. Matthew felt too much for Kit.

"No one comes before you." He held Kit's stare as he made the claim, hoping Kit understood he meant it.

The insulted stammering coming from the doorway became a distraction. Matthew's gaze shot toward the door. "We're busy." He kicked the door closed.

Kit stared at Matthew's mouth.

Matthew couldn't have been harder.

"Your hands are on my ass."

Matthew licked his lips. He swore he could already taste Kit. "Your ass is in my hands."

Kit leaned a hair closer. "That's fair."

A stuttered breath escaped Matthew.

He felt Kit go hard against him.

Matthew broke. He backed Kit against the door and claimed Kit's mouth. Kit came back at him every bit as hard. Matthew let Kit's feet slide to the floor so he could grasp Kit's jaw. He held Kit's face in place so he could lick Kit's tongue exactly the way he had dreamed of doing.

His pants loosened and Matthew knew he had to slow things down. He wouldn't last long once Kit touched his dick. "Let's take this to the bedroom."

A soft pant escaped Kit. "I might change my mind if you stop now."

Matthew couldn't let that happen. He was too close now, but this was important too. "I'm not doing this here and hurting you."

"I'm used to being hurt."

Matthew swept Kit from his feet. "Not on my watch." He hurried through the house and to the bedroom. The instant he set Kit on the bed, he went to work, keeping Kit on fire. He kissed Kit's stomach and lightly traced Kit's erection through his underwear. Matthew only leaned away in small bursts, removing items of clothing and going for the lube and condoms.

By the time Matthew had stripped away their clothes and suited up, he was way too close to the edge. He stroked Kit's cock while praying Kit was as close as he was, or Matthew might disappoint him. Matthew fingered Kit, massaging that hot spot while stretching him. He wanted Kit to come back for more. His mind was too big of a mess for foreplay.

Kit shoved at his chest. Matthew's heart dropped. Kit had tried warning him. It seemed Matthew had taken too long and Kit's mind had changed. Even though it killed him, Matthew stopped.

"I'm sorry. Am I scaring you?" Matthew knew he felt too much when it came to Kit. He always turned too dark for anyone's comfort.

Kit didn't respond. He kept pushing and shoving until he had Matthew on his back. Kit kept coming until he straddled Matthew's hips. He grabbed Matthew's dick, held it in place, and then sat on it. Matthew's body jackknifed from the bed. He had to grab the headboard to hold himself in place. His eyes rolled back in his head. He wanted this too much and for too long. Kit looked beautiful sitting on Matthew's cock.

He held still and stared down at Matthew with flushed cheeks. As Matthew looked on, Kit jacked off while his asshole tried sucking Matthew deeper. Kit didn't hide his feelings. He gasped and moaned while tugging his cock. Pressure climbed Matthew's shaft as he watched Kit pleasuring himself. Kit's performance was a million times hotter than any porn Matthew had ever watched.

Kit's head fell backward. He rocked himself on Matthew's dick. Kit stroked faster, riding his palm. Matthew stayed completely still, frozen by his fantasies coming to life. Kit's chin dropped. His gaze collided with Matthew's. Kit looked more aroused than Matthew could have imagined. His lips were swollen and parted. He was the single most gorgeous sight Matthew had ever set eyes upon. Matthew couldn't look away.

A loud gasp burst from Kit and hot cum hit Matthew in the chin. Matthew's stomach concaved as ecstasy slammed into him. He fought for air as he desperately tried holding on to the moment forever. Matthew bit his tongue to stop words from flowing from his lips. He was completely in love with Kit and had been for much longer than he could ever admit. Matthew never thought he would be with Kit like this. It was beautiful. He couldn't turn back now.

*

With darkness surrounding them, Kit kept his ear pressed to Matthew's chest. He loved the sound of Matthew's heart beating against his ear and the way Matthew kept running his fingers down the back of Kit's arm. It was such a pleasant moment. Kit didn't get to have this.

"How can you afford this house?" Kit had no idea why he whispered the question. It was so dark, and the moment felt intimate. He didn't want to break the spell, but he also needed to know Matthew's secrets. He felt like they were going places. Kit wanted every piece of Matthew.

"My parents were killed in a car accident when I was four. My grandfather raised me. When he died, I inherited all this and then some."

Huh. Kit couldn't explain it, but Matthew's story seemed a little too simple. Since he didn't know how to say that without sounding like an asshole, he didn't say anything at all.

"I told you my story. Now it's your turn. Why are you choosing to stay with Frost and Zep?"

"Maybe I don't like living alone. Why is my living situation so weird to you?"

Matthew huffed. "Why are you so prickly all the time? For fuck's sake, just tell me your story and then it'll be done. You'll never have to say it again. I just want to know you better." Matthew tilted Kit's chin up so Kit couldn't avoid his stare. "We're supposed to want to tell each other everything."

"What do you want to hear?" Kit asked in aggravation. The peace was gone now. "Do you need me to say that I'm scared to sleep in a house alone? Do you want me to say I had a huge fight with my raging alcoholic mom at twelve? Then when I stormed out and started walking down the road, I found myself in the car with an old man who drove me to Texas, where I spent the next three years acting as his bratty boy until I poisoned his food and watched him choke on his vomit. Afterward, I took eighty thousand from his safe and made my way to L.A., where I haven't let another man touch me sexually again until tonight. Is that what you expect to hear?" Even Kit heard the exasperation and the disingenuousness in his voice. He couldn't help it. Kit didn't know how to be whatever it was Matthew wanted so badly from him. Matthew didn't want the real him. Hell, Kit wasn't even sure if Kit knew the real him anymore.

Maybe the empty shell that surviving had left behind was all he was anymore. Maybe there really wasn't anything left of him on the inside. He couldn't tell that story with his genuine emotions shining through. That might break him in a way that Kit wouldn't survive.

Matthew stared at him for so long that Kit wanted to scream. Finally, Matthew released a soft sigh. "I guess I'll have to work harder to make you trust me enough to tell me the truth someday."

Kit bit back an aggravated huff. It was for the best. If Matthew had believed him, then Kit would have to live with knowing he was the reason Matthew looked at him differently. Only two other people in the world had ever heard that story. They both only looked at him with pity afterward. This had been an amazing night until now. Kit would treasure it. But he had a feeling it was time for him to move on from this town. He had been here too long. Three people too many knew his truth. Canada had some great film studios. Maybe he would go there. Damn, he was tired. No one had any idea how exhausting it was to pretend every second of the day. When he was alone with his books, that was the only time his brain got any rest. Unfortunately, the more time he spent with Matthew, the more Kit realized he couldn't be with anyone. He couldn't share his life and keep his secrets.

Despite his decision to leave, Kit's hold tightened on Matthew. He would give himself until Matthew fell asleep. Then he would disappear. He should have known Matthew was too good to be true. Kit wouldn't forget again.

Chapter Three

Kit's phone was on the bedside table. That was what fucked with Matthew the most. It had been two days and Kit hadn't come looking for it. He didn't show for yoga. Matthew hadn't seen him at Frost's. By day three, Matthew was out of his head. He finally broke and headed to Frost's, looking for answers.

Zep was alone with the twins when Matthew arrived. He glanced Matthew's way as Matthew slipped inside the kitchen.

"Hey. I didn't know you were stopping by today. Kit isn't here."

Matthew stooped and greeted the girls with hugs and kisses before responding. "Yeah. I didn't see his SUV outside, but that's sort of why I stopped by. Do you have a minute?"

Zep turned off the water and wiped his hands on his jeans. "Sure. Is everything okay?"

Matthew shrugged. "I don't really know where to start other than to just jump right in. A few nights ago, Kit told me a story about his past. I thought he was just fucking around to get me to stop asking, but..."

Zep winced.

Matthew's heart dropped at Zep's expression. Matthew hadn't wanted to worry him. He just wanted to find Kit. "Shit. Everything he said was true."

"Kit never lies. He's painfully honest with everyone all the time. Even if he covers his words in snark or flirting, he means them. Honestly, I'm blown away that he told you. He doesn't tell anyone that story."

Matthew kept playing the part, hoping for any extra info he could get. "For real, if you'd heard him tell me that story, he sounded exactly like he made some shit up on the fly to get me to stop asking. I didn't think anything else about it until he stopped showing up."

Zep's eyebrows rose. "What do you mean he stopped showing up?"

Matthew shrugged again. He felt ridiculous as hell—like he had turned into a full-fledged stalker. "You know, he quit coming to yoga. He left his phone at my place and I thought he would come back for it, but nope. He just disappeared from the planet."

Zep rushed for the stairs. His reaction was so sudden, Matthew didn't know if he should run after him or watch the girls. In the end, he stood there like an idiot and waited. Zep was easily six-six and looked like a biker daddy. Matthew would have never thought the guy could move that quick.

"He's gone," Zep said, reappearing. "It looks like he took everything. What should I do? Should I file a missing person's report? Is that an option even available to me?"

Zep sounded so panicked that Matthew felt like shit for dragging him into things.

Zep's alarm didn't subside. "I knew he hadn't been home in a few days, but I thought he was with you, since he's always with you. You say he didn't even take his phone. Holy shit. Do you think he plans to harm himself?"

Matthew made a calming gesture, even though Zep's fear began feeding his own. "I have some friends who work for the LAPD. I'll give them a

47

call and we'll get this figured out." Matthew didn't think Kit would harm himself. He thought Kit was running away. Matthew couldn't have that. Kit belonged to him. Matthew would get him back if it was the last thing he ever did. If he couldn't, it definitely would be the last thing he ever did. Kit was the only thing left tying him to this life. Matthew was nowhere near sane enough to keep going if Kit was gone.

*

San Francisco didn't have that spark Kit searched for, so tonight was his last night. Tomorrow, he would move farther north and pick a new spot. If that didn't hold his interest, then Canada would be next. He didn't know what would make him happy. Kit couldn't stay in hotels forever, but he didn't like being in a house alone. In a hotel, even though he was alone in a room, he knew he could call out for help. Someone would hear. In a house, he would be isolated with his terror.

Kit moved from suitcase to suitcase, repacking his things. He wore nothing beneath his short robe. That meant less to pack tomorrow. Kit needed to find a bookstore that sold and traded books. He'd finished his last paperback tonight and needed something new. Since he always traveled light, he had to trade his old ones to keep them from weighing him down. As he closed the lid on his suitcase, his hotel room door opened. Kit didn't have time to be scared before recognizing his intruder. The moment Kit caught sight of Matthew, he realized he had been waiting for Matthew to find him. Matthew always did.

"I think we need to talk about your constant

stalking. You have a problem."

Matthew didn't look the least bit guilty. "You left me."

Kit couldn't deny the shiver that ran down his spine. He had known Matthew would chase him. Even though Kit couldn't explain how he knew, Kit counted on Matthew never letting him go. He needed Matthew to prove himself. Despite his hard shell, Kit was a mess on the inside. He needed someone a little crazy to hold him together.

"I do that sometimes."

Matthew moved closer. His gaze never wavered from Kit, making Kit tense. He knew Matthew would pounce any second. "Not anymore, you don't. You agreed we're a couple. That means no more running away. That means you're mine."

Kit nervously licked his lips. He didn't know

what to say. He had already told Matthew why he was fucked up, but Matthew hadn't believed him. There was no point in rehashing the story. He decided to go with a different truth.

"You knew I was a mess before you took me to bed."

Matthew took off his shirt. "Pick your punishment."

Kit's eyebrows shot to his hairline. "Fuck that bullshit. If you don't want to deal with my flightiness, you shouldn't have messed with me. If you fall for a crazy hot mess, that's what you'll always get."

Matthew didn't appear to listen. He dug through Kit's things until he found some lube. He set it on the table and went to work on stripping away the rest of his clothes. "Fine, if you won't choose, I will. Apologize or you'll never touch me again."

Kit blinked. He had no idea how to react. That odd punishment hadn't even been on his radar. A spanking, maybe. Never touching Matthew again, nope. That wasn't an option for him.

Once Matthew was completely nude, he sat in a chair at the table and squirted some lube in his hand. As Kit looked on, Matthew stroked his cock, getting hard.

Kit sat on the edge of the bed. His gaze wouldn't budge from Matthew's erection. Lube made his cock shine. Kit's mouth watered. "It doesn't look like you need me."

Matthew's gaze hooded. He watched Kit with a hunger that was almost tangible. "You only have so long, Kit. Once I come, you've lost your chance.

I'm walking out and you're never touching me again."

His body was on fire. Matthew was the sexiest man on the planet to Kit. Kit couldn't stop watching him. A flush rose on Matthew's cheeks. Kit swallowed. For years, Kit had loathed the thought of anyone touching him. In fact, the idea made him sick. He had never been attracted to anyone until Matthew. In a year of friendship, something had grown inside Kit. Matthew was the only person he wanted. Maybe that terrified him more than he wanted to admit. Still, he couldn't lose Matthew just because Kit had been scared for a moment.

"Hurry, Kit. I can't wait forever."

Maybe he would shrivel up and die if Matthew never touched him again. "I'm sorry."

Matthew exploded from his chair and tackled

Kit to the bed. Kit didn't have time to breathe. Matthew's tongue was in his mouth. The two halves of Kit's robe parted. Matthew moved against Kit's body, making love to him with no penetration. The friction between their bodies drove Kit insane. He fought to get closer. Kit pulled Matthew's hair and bit at his lips. He was wild with need. Nothing mattered but the release Matthew offered. When his orgasm hit, Kit cried out against Matthew's mouth.

Matthew tore his mouth away and roared as he came. It was the sexiest sight Kit had ever witnessed. He dropped his forehead to Kit's shoulder and gasped for air. Kit stroked his back and his hair. His eyes stung. Kit was damaged beyond repair. He had known that for a long time. No one had ever fought to stay with him. Kit never imagined anyone would. Matthew had. He had shown up. Kit needed him.

Matthew kissed Kit's shoulder. "You're mine. Don't run away again. I'll always find you."

Kit's hold tightened on Matthew. There was no way Matthew could possibly know. Kit needed his crazy, persistent strength. There was a very good chance Kit would get spooked again. Matthew had to be the strong one.

*

Matthew couldn't stop holding Kit and kissing him. Everything Kit owned was inside this hotel room. He hadn't intended to come back. Matthew couldn't let him get away. He knew he was insane. It was only a matter of time before Kit found out just how much. There was no sense in hiding the worst of himself.

"What was your plan?"

He felt Kit shrug. "I didn't have one."

Oddly, Matthew found comfort in that. Kit had blindly run away. He hadn't meticulously plotted his escape from Matthew. Matthew kissed Kit's chest. "You should let Zep know you're okay. He was ready to fill out a missing person's report."

"Oh no. Poor Zep. I didn't mean to scare him."

Matthew didn't feel an ounce of shame. Kit needed a lecture. "You have people who love you. Leaving without a word isn't an option. If you need a break, say so. Not from me, though. You're stuck with me."

Kit chuckled. He scratched Matthew's head, making his eyelids feel heavy. Matthew forced his eyes back open. The last time he had fallen asleep with Kit, Kit had run for the hills.

"I'll call Zep, but what then?"

Matthew came up onto his elbow and met Kit's stare. "What do you mean, what then? Then you're coming home with me and you'll be happy and never scare me like this again."

Kit pursed his lips, as if thinking that one over. "I suppose you are closer to my hairstylist than Zep's."

Matthew fought a smile. Kit was such a pain. He couldn't just say he wanted to be with Matthew. Matthew loved it. "See? I'm already making your life easier."

Kit suddenly turned serious. "I don't think you know what you're getting into. You've never lived with me. I have nightmares. Sometimes, I don't sleep for days to avoid them. I'll just go until I drop. You don't know the broken side of me."

Yes, he did, because Matthew was every bit as

fucked up. "I'm here for it. Give me your worst. I'm not blind or deaf. I hear what you're saying, but I'm not scared. You're stunning, but that's not why I can't stay away. I love being with you. The real you."

For a moment, Kit's gaze moved over Matthew's face, as if looking for any lie. Finally, he shook his head—like giving up. "Don't be insulted if I don't unpack my bags."

"I won't, but don't think for a second I'll let you go either."

A smile exploded across Kit's face. "I don't understand you at all. You're completely insane for wanting this."

Matthew linked his fingers through Kit's. His gaze never wavered from holding Kit's stare. He wanted Kit to see the truth in every word he spoke.

"I am insane, but not for loving you."

Kit's smile turned surprisingly shy. He brought Matthew's hand to his mouth and kissed his wrist right beneath his palm. His gaze locked on Matthew's wrist and didn't budge. Matthew fought the urge to yank his hand away. Kit traced the scars his tattoos usually kept hidden. He shoved at Matthew's chest until he had Matthew on his back so Kit could straddle his hips. Kit inspected his other arm. Matthew couldn't breathe as he stared at Kit. To Matthew's shock, Kit's eyes filled with tears as he obviously came to terms with exactly how many times Matthew had failed at killing himself. Fear choked him. He couldn't tell Kit why. He wasn't strong like Kit.

Kit kissed his wrists before meeting Matthew's gaze. "Never again. Understood?"

"I'm not going anywhere. I promise." Matthew held Kit's stare as he made the vow. He meant every word. Kit needed him to be the steady one. Matthew wouldn't fail him… he hoped.

Chapter Four

Zep glared at Kit over the edge of his coffee cup. Kit knew the only reason Zep hadn't torn into him yet was because the girls were there. That was why Kit kept playing with them. Since Matthew had brought Kit's phone with him to San Francisco, Kit had done the chicken shit thing and texted Zep to let Zep know he was fine. He had also claimed he would explain when he stopped by today. So far, he hadn't done much beyond drinking pretend tea with Zep's daughters.

Kit couldn't take the tension any longer. He decided to go with a safe topic: Zep's unborn baby. "So... has Lori found out yet what your new baby will be?"

"The ultrasound is next week. Matthew, please

take the girls to go find some cookies for their tea."

Squeals rent the air as Matthew raced the girls into the kitchen. Kit stared at Matthew's retreating back and silently dubbed him a traitor.

The moment they were alone, Zep exploded. "What in the hell were you thinking? Anything could've happened to you and you didn't even take your phone. I know you're used to setting out on your own, but you have people who—"

"I love you."

Zep's shoulders fell at Kit's interruption. "I love you too."

He didn't want to make excuses, but he also needed to talk. "Matthew and I had sex."

Zep visibly tried hiding his shock. He set his coffee cup aside. Kit nearly laughed at his obvious attempt to seem calm.

Kit didn't wait for Zep to ask all the questions he likely wanted to ask. "I got scared."

"Then you should have—"

Kit made a calming gesture, cutting Zep off again. "You know me. You know my story. I know I should have come to you, but I'm not used to having anyone care about me. Occasionally, I will fail at this having people in my life thing, but I'm trying."

Zep's gaze shot to where Matthew hung out with the twins in the kitchen, as if checking to ensure he had time to talk. "Are you sure you can handle this?"

A snort escaped Kit. "Not at all." He shrugged. "It doesn't matter, though. I love him. I have to try."

"Awww."

Kit rolled his eyes. Zep was such a squishy

bear. "Don't get all mushy on me. We've been pretty much dating for a year now. I guess it was inevitable that I would feel something eventually." He wasn't good at talking about his feelings. Kit heard how flippant he sounded. All he could do was hope Zep saw through his bullshit—the way he always did.

Zep looked thoughtful. "You know, I'm really impressed with this guy. He looks like such a bad boy. Yet he waited for a whole year to get in your pants, and then he chased after you when you ran. I think you should marry him now before he gets away. Not everyone has the patience for a demisexual."

Kit's gaze slid toward Matthew. A chuckle rose in Kit's throat as he watched Matthew pretend to eat the girls' cookies, making them squeal in protest.

"He's pretty spectacular. That's what makes him so terrifying. I could really hurt this one."

"So don't."

A smile snapped to Kit's lips as he met Zep's stare again. "Just like that, huh?"

Zep shrugged. "It'll take work. There will be lots of times that you'll have to stop, take a breath, and force yourself to think before acting. But if he's worth it to you, then you'll do it, and it'll get easier. I know your instinct is to run when things get hard. That's how you've survived, and I love you for always pulling through. Times have changed though, baby. You have people who love you. Like it or not, you've planted seeds that turned into roots in this town. You're stuck tending all of us now."

"God, you're such a parent."

Zep smiled, looking completely unashamed. "I

know, and I fully expect a gift from you on Father's Day."

Kit sniffed. "Fine, but it'll be terrible. I'm talking ties, coffee mugs, and socks for days."

A deep rumble of laughter came from Zep's chest. "And I'll love it all because it came from you."

Kit's throat suddenly swelled. He had to look away. Kit did as Zep suggested. He took a breath and forced himself to stay put. It was so much easier to run when he felt too much. Kit really hoped he didn't fail all these people he had tricked into loving him. He was nowhere near as stable as he led them to believe. That was pretty fucking pathetic.

*

Kit was a little too quiet and still on the way home. That was very un-Kit-like. Unless Kit had a book in his hand, he was a ball of nonstop energy. He was always on the move, joining Matthew at the gym, or on the hunt for new modeling gigs or movie roles. After speaking to Zep alone, Kit seemed drained.

Even though Matthew knew Kit would lie and claim he was fine, he still had to ask. "Are you okay?"

"I'm not lovable," Kit answered immediately—like the words had been hanging on the tip of his tongue all day.

Still, Matthew hadn't expected that.

"Really. I'm not even likable."

Matthew fought a laugh. "I think we'll have to agree to disagree on this one."

Kit didn't back down. "I'm being serious. What's wrong with all of you?"

After steering Kit's SUV down the driveway,

Matthew killed the engine and focused on Kit. "Where is all this coming from?"

Kit shrugged. "I'm just confused, I guess. Some people are really nice, like Zep. Other people are super charming like you. I get why people like Zep and you. It doesn't make sense for anyone to like me based on my personality unless you're a masochist."

Matthew unbuckled his seatbelt and jumped from the vehicle. He circled the SUV and opened Kit's door before he could get away. Kit turned his way, as if he intended to get out. Matthew crowded Kit's space until he stood between Kit's knees. He snagged Kit's waist and hauled Kit forward. Kit's arms encircled Matthew's neck.

"Look at me."

A smile snapped to Kit's face. "I am."

With a shake of his head, Matthew tried harder to make Kit understand. "I mean, look closely at me. See me."

Kit's smile slipped away as his gaze moved over Matthew's face.

"What do you see?" Matthew asked, while not hiding a single emotion.

Kit visibly swallowed, as if his throat hurt. "I don't know."

"Yes, you do. What do you see?"

Each second that ticked by, Kit looked a little more panicked. "I don't want to say."

Matthew kissed Kit's cheek. "Come on, Kitty. Tell me what you feel when I'm staring at you."

He heard Kit take a ragged breath. "Loved. I feel loved."

"Damn straight." Matthew kissed Kit with

every bit of love he felt in his heart. By the time he pulled away, Matthew's heart beat a little too fast. He pressed his forehead to Kit's and held his stare. "It isn't your job to be lovable. You already are because you have people who already love you. It's not your choice. You're not responsible for other people's thoughts and feelings. People feel how they feel and there's nothing you can do about it. The only thing you can control is how you react to those feelings. Got it?"

"Okay."

Damn. Matthew didn't deserve the trust and faith Kit showed him. "How do you plan to react?"

Kit touched his lips to Matthew's. For a moment, he stayed like that—lips barely brushing while sharing each other's air. "I'll love you back," Kit finally responded in a whisper. It sounded like a shout to Matthew's ears. He held Kit tighter and deepened their kiss. Things turned heated faster than he intended until they were full-on making out in the driveway. Matthew had no sense when it came to Kit. He wanted Kit in every sense. Mostly, he craved spending the rest of his life like this, soaking up Kit's love and pretending he was Matthew Ross. Matthew knew he wouldn't get forever once Kit found out he wasn't.

"There are kids in this neighborhood."

At the grouchy and condescending chastisement, Kit chuckled against Matthew's lips. "Why is she always so goddamn far from her house?"

At Kit's whispered question, Matthew matched his hushed tone. "I think she's secretly a voyeur."

Kit's body shook with silent laughter. "We

should buy a giant Pride flag for the yard. Our house would be the talk of the neighborhood."

Kit had called it their house. Matthew's throat swelled. He had never wanted anything more than this dream he had built on lies. "Let's do that. First, let's go cuddle."

Matthew tightened his hold on Kit. Kit took the hint and wrapped his legs around Matthew, holding on. Matthew headed for the door with Kit clinging to him like a monkey. He would take every moment he got with Kit and pray he never got caught in his own web. That was all the plan Matthew had right now. He was living for the moment. The present was all he had. Matthew didn't know how to live any other way.

Chapter Five

One of Kit's favorite things with Matthew was being at the gym with him. As a personal trainer and yoga instructor for Fitness Titan—a gym owned by Zep's husband Frost—Matthew spent a lot of time at the gym. Kit had always been a small guy, but he had to stay as close to perfect as possible for modeling gigs. That was easier than ever, thanks to dating Matthew. Kit took Matthew's every yoga class. In between classes, they would sit on their mats and talk, or play. Matthew found every hiding spot in the place to steal moments alone with Kit. Kit loved being with Matthew nonstop. That had never happened to him before.

"I should give you a job. You're always here," Frost said as he came through the door of Fitness

Titan. He struggled to keep up with the twins.

Kit automatically helped out by taking Millie's hand. He spoke to the girls first. "Good morning, gorgeous ladies. How are you?"

The girls spoke over each other, trying to one-up the other as they showed off the toys they had brought with them. It took Kit a minute to get back to Frost's comment. "I have no interest in a normal job, but thank you. Is Zep working?"

Frost led the way to his office and spoke over his shoulder. "Yeah. He's about to leave, though. If you're here in the next half hour, you'll see him. He plans to stop by to get the girls on his way home."

"Oh, okay." He had done his friendship duty, so he felt like he should go. Frost was a good guy and Kit—reluctantly—liked him, but they weren't as close as Kit was with Zep. "Well, I guess I should leave you to your work."

Frost stopped him before he could get away. "Actually, if you don't mind, can you hang out with these two for a couple of minutes while I run to the bathroom?"

"Sure." Kit loved the twins. They were no chore. "Go. I'm good to hang out here."

Frost didn't hang around for Kit to his change his mind. Kit got it. He knew taking care of small kids was no easy feat. Frost probably never got to go to the bathroom.

Matthew appeared in the doorway. The girls squealed and ran to meet him. He dropped to his haunches and hugged them while patiently listening to all the same stories Kit had heard already this morning. Apparently, they were excited about these light-up fans their grammie had bought them. Kit couldn't stop watching the interaction. Matthew genuinely cared what the girls had to say. It was obvious he cared about them. The moment struck Kit in a way he couldn't articulate. He felt too much at one time. Kit could see the goodness in Matthew, and he was proud to know Matthew belonged to him. At the same time, he was completely terrified because Matthew was a great man and he had tied himself to Kit.

"You're amazing with them."

Matthew glanced up and smiled. "They're kids. They haven't learned to look for the worst in people yet. It's refreshing."

"Do you want kids?"

Something passed over Matthew's features. It was gone before Kit could decipher Matthew's thoughts. "No." He went back to playing with the spinning fans with the girls.

Even though Kit was relieved Matthew didn't want kids, since he didn't either, there was still something bothering him. It was the way Matthew had said no. It was almost hard—like something dark drove his refusal. There were times when Kit felt like he didn't know Matthew at all. In some ways, he didn't. They never talked about their pasts, which was perfect as far as Kit was concerned. Still, living in the present wasn't always simple. Kit wanted every side of Matthew, maybe most especially his secrets.

Frost reappeared. "Whew. Thank you. You have no idea how hard it is to get a bathroom break with two little girls."

Kit forced a smile to his lips. "Matthew did all the entertaining, so no problem. I guess I should get back to my workout."

Kit and Matthew spent several more minutes trying to leave while the girls fought to keep them there. By the time Kit closed Frost's office door, he felt like he had already finished his workout.

"Whoa. I don't know how they do it. That's a lot of work."

Matthew chuckled. "Just think. In a few months, they'll have another one."

Kit shook his head. He couldn't fathom being tied down like that. Kit much preferred being selfish. He liked reading for hours and going wherever he wanted whenever he wanted to go. Being a parent wasn't for him. Not to mention, Kit was completely fucked up and had no business being in charge of keeping another soul alive. He was so caught up in his thoughts that it took Kit a moment to realize how quiet Matthew was being.

"Are you okay?"

Matthew flashed him a bright smile. "Of course. I have you."

The funny thing was, in spite of Matthew's sudden disappearance inside himself, Kit still believed Matthew. He was completely fine because he had Kit. Kit linked fingers with him and skipped toward the yoga room, making Matthew laugh as he joined in. Everything was perfect. They had each other.

*

Everything was perfect. It was better than excellent. Matthew had never known so much happiness. There were still moments of blinding PTSD, but being with Kit made everything better. He hadn't known life could be like this.

Kit helped him set up mats. Then they did a few stretching exercises before settling down to breathe. With his spine straight and the bottoms of his feet touching, Kit sat with his eyes closed. He looked peaceful. Matthew knew he should be focusing on taking mindful breaths. He couldn't. His eyes refused to shut against Kit. Kit was perfect. His light brown hair was impeccably styled despite a morning of exercise. He had lips that begged to be savored. Even his long lashes fascinated Matthew. After Kit's question about whether Matthew wanted kids, Matthew now realized they didn't talk about the future. That was on Matthew. Talking about the future felt every bit as dangerous as talking about the past. Matthew didn't know which way to go.

Matthew had been trying so hard to focus on the now that he hadn't considered where they were headed. He was afraid to dream. Matthew had never seen a future for himself. He didn't know how to plan for one with Kit. The thing was, though, Matthew wanted a permanent life with Kit. Kit had been living with him for two months now, and every day was immaculate.

While Kit focused on his breathing, Matthew silently shifted to his knees. His gaze never wavered from Kit. A half second before Matthew sprang, Kit's sexy brown eyes opened and latched on to him. Matthew tackled him to the floor. Peals of laughter bounced from the walls as Matthew playfully nuzzled Kit's body, trying to tickle him.

"No. Stop. I don't like to be tickled."

Matthew went obnoxiously still on top of Kit, squashing him to the floor. "Okay. I won't move."

Kit halfheartedly shoved at Matthew's chest.

"You're too heavy. You'll flatten me."

"You told me to stop."

He could feel Kit's laughter. "Fine. You win. I concede. You're bigger and stronger."

Matthew shifted his weight to his hands and knees. "I don't believe it. You're strong as hell. You could take me, if you wanted."

Kit bit his bottom lip.

"Goddamn." The whispered curse slipped from Matthew without thought. Looking at Kit always wowed him. He couldn't believe Kit was here with him.

Kit pushed and twisted, flipping Matthew onto his back. A bright smile lit his face as he straddled Matthew's body. Matthew blinked, trying to figure out how he ended up on his back. Kit never stopped amazing him. "Marry me."

Kit threw his head back and roared with laughter.

Matthew didn't back down. "I'm serious. Marry me."

Kit dropped his chin. His eyes still swam with laughter. "You don't want to be tied to my craziness forever."

"Yes, I do. Marry me."

The laughter in Kit's expression slowly slipped away as the truth seemed to set in. "Oh. You really are serious."

Matthew slipped his hands up Kit's thighs. "I am. I knew when I met you last year that you were one of a kind. Every day since, that feeling has grown. There's no one else for me." Kit had no idea how true that last bit was. Matthew couldn't and wouldn't share his life with anyone else.

The door to the yoga room opened and Kit scrambled away. Matthew sat up with his heart beating loudly in his ears. He needed Kit's answer, but he also knew it would be no. At least Kit knew now where Matthew stood. He knew Matthew was in this for as long as Kit would stay.

Matthew went through the motions, teaching his class. He tried not to look at Kit too much. There was a real chance he had scared Kit with his question. When the class came to an end, Matthew dragged his feet while cleaning away the mess. Kit seemed to be equally avoiding Matthew as he helped. When they were done and Matthew couldn't ignore Kit any longer, he turned to find Kit calmly waiting.

"I guess we should go home and shower."

Matthew tried to hide his nervousness by

falling back on humor. "Are you saying I stink?"

Kit looked adorably confused. "No. I just didn't think you'd want to get married in our gym clothes."

Matthew blinked, and then he blinked some more. His brain didn't want to accept Kit's words. Finally, his mouth took a chance. "I would marry you in anything at all, but I see your point. We're only doing this once, so we should look nice."

Kit's expression was oddly serene, as if he had no doubts. "That was my thought as well."

A slow smile stretched Matthew's lips. He wanted to shout his happiness at the top of his lungs. Instead, he quietly took Kit's hand and brought it to his lips before heading for the door. Matthew had no intention of looking a gift horse in the mouth. Kit agreed to marry him. Matthew wasn't looking back.

*

Life felt strangely normal. Kit watched as Matthew locked Kit's birth certificate and social security card in the safe alongside his and their new marriage certificate. Everything should feel surreal or crazy, but no. Somewhere along the line, they had built this super ordinary life that felt steady and right. Kit had no regrets.

Kit sat on Matthew's desk, riding the high of his happiness. "How long should we wait to call Zep and Frost?"

Matthew showed Kit how to open the safe a second time, as if he thought Kit would forget. "The code is pretty easy to remember if you need your things. We can call them now if you'd like."

The longer Kit stared at Matthew, the more the truth sank in. This was his husband. Someone had claimed him as their family. Husband wasn't a fake title Kit had given him because he loved him. This was real. Those tattooed hands that Kit always craved having on his skin, they were his now. This guy who everyone craved belonged to Kit. A sudden burst of uncontrollable happiness surged through Kit. He climbed to his feet on top of Matthew's desk and held his arms wide.

"I'm your husband." The words came out in a loud shout.

Matthew laughed. "You definitely are. Don't fall."

"You should come up here with me. We can be on top of the world together." Matthew had a large and solid oak desk that was way too fancy. Kit wasn't worried about it holding two adults' weight.

Matthew stood. Instead of joining Kit on the

desk, he ran his hands up the backs of Kit's legs. "I've been on top of the world since the day I met you. Today, I'm a fucking king. Come here."

Kit bent and braced his hands on Matthew's shoulders.

Matthew plucked him from the desk. The moment Kit's feet were on solid ground, he dug Kit's phone from his pocket. After flashing the face Kit's way to unlock the device, he called Zep on speaker phone.

Zep answered on the second ring. "Hello?"

Kit couldn't stop smiling. "Hey, sweetie. Do you have a minute?"

"Of course. What's up?"

"You're on speaker phone and Matthew is here. We have something kind of crazy to tell you."

"Okay." Zep dragged out the word, sounding

confused.

"We got married," Matthew shouted before Kit could say anything else.

"That's amazing. I'm so happy for you both. I'm a little shocked, but not in a bad way."

"I'm still a little shocked too," Kit admitted. "But not in a bad way. You know me, though. I don't play coy. If I want something, I don't hesitate." He held Matthew's stare. "I wanted this."

"I can't tell you how happy I am. You deserve all the happiness in the world. Not to steal your thunder, but I have news too. We had our ultrasound yesterday."

Kit held his breath. Things went wrong sometimes at ultrasounds, and Zep really wanted more kids. "And?"

"To our delight and surprise, we'll be

welcoming another set of twin girls."

Kit yanked the phone from Matthew's hand. "Holy shit. Are you kidding me?"

Zep laughed. "Nope. We're about to be completely overrun by girls in our house."

Kit's throat swelled. "They're the luckiest kids in the world."

Zep read too much into Kit's choked words. "There will always be room for you here too."

Matthew stared at Kit a little too hard. Kit couldn't take this much scrutinizing from the only people he loved. "Don't worry about me. I have a family too now." He met Matthew's gaze again as he made the claim. He felt the words all the way to his soul. "I'll let you get back to the girls. Congrats on the twins."

"Congratulations on the marriage. Let's get

together tomorrow."

Kit could barely think with Matthew staring at him with so much possessiveness in his eyes. "Sounds great. I love you."

"Love you too. Bye."

"Bye." Kit set the phone aside.

Matthew massaged Kit's hips between his hands, drawing Kit closer. "No matter how many times I turn the day over in my head, I still can't believe you're mine."

Kit linked his fingers behind Matthew's neck. "Like I said, I don't hold back when I want something. I wanted this marriage."

"I want you."

Butterflies stirred in Kit's stomach. "Then why don't you stop talking about it and start being about it."

Matthew backed Kit against the desk. He looked intense as hell. Kit wanted whatever came next. "Take off your shirt."

Kit took off his shirt.

In one swift move, Matthew lifted Kit from the floor and set him on the desk. "On your back."

Kit immediately obeyed, stretching out across the desk.

Matthew went to work on Kit's pants. "This is probably a bad time for a story, especially one that might make you regret marrying me. You're getting one anyhow." Matthew peeled away Kit's pants and underwear. "I'm a recovering addict."

Kit hadn't expected that one. His body didn't care. Matthew set him on fire.

Matthew kept talking while toying with Kit's body. "A couple of years ago, things had gotten to their lowest point. I walked into a convenience store with a loaded handgun, determined to force the cops to shoot me dead. While I waited for the store to empty of customers, I picked up a magazine."

Kit was split right down the middle. This was a tremendous revelation. Yet Matthew had him too enthralled by his touch to react.

Matthew bent and kissed Kit's hipbone. "When I flipped it open, you were inside."

Kit blinked. He definitely hadn't been expecting that.

Matthew dragged his tongue up Kit's erection before continuing. "The sight of you stunned me. All thought left me. My high disappeared. I had never seen a more beautiful sight than you. You saved me that day."

Kit swallowed. He didn't know what to say.

Matthew didn't wait for him to find words. "I went to rehab and got my shit together." Matthew stared down at Kit with more intensity than Kit had ever witnessed. "The day I spotted you inside Fitness Titan, I knew I would marry you. It was like fate had dangled a picture of you in my face, letting me know what my prize would be if I could find my way back. Then there you were. You were always meant for me."

Tears filled Kit's eyes. It was like Matthew's story explained so much. He had always felt as if they were connected somehow. Matthew had never felt like a stranger. From the moment they met, it had been as if they had known each other their entire lives. This was fate. Matthew was right. They were meant to meet.

"I believe."

At Kit's whispered words, the possessiveness in Matthew's expression doubled. He tugged Kit's hips forward and sucked Kit's dick. There was no sweet make-out session. Matthew was on Kit's dick, licking and sucking. Swallowing him whole. Kit couldn't do anything but clutch at Matthew's shoulders and try not to come immediately. He wanted to savor the moment. No one made him feel powerful the way Matthew did. Kit felt normal. No one understood the power in that.

Matthew pulled away, making Kit whimper. He opened a desk drawer and came out with lube.

"Why in the fuck do you have lube in your desk drawer?" Even to Kit's ears, he sounded breathless rather than angry.

Matthew chuckled. "Don't worry, sexy. No one else has ever been fucked on this desk. The doorknob kept sticking in here. A guy from work told me to try lube. It got left in here afterward. That's all. You're the only guy I've ever brought home."

Kit sniffed. "I'm the only one you'll ever be with again."

Matthew's hungry gaze met Kit's. "Damn straight." His lubed fingers probed Kit's asshole. Their gazes never wavered. Kit was different with Matthew. He wanted things he had never craved with anyone else. His eyes fell closed as Matthew's cock stretched him wide. He breathed through the pleasure and the pain. His mind stayed right there with Matthew. This was his husband. They had really done it. A weight Kit had carried for so long he had forgotten he carried it fell away. For once, he could breathe. This was the first day of a new everything. Kit was finally home.

Chapter Six

One thing Matthew had gotten accustomed to—while teaching yoga in L.A.—was having celebrities in his class. For the most part, Matthew didn't notice anymore. He wanted everyone to keep coming back. If someone famous felt like they couldn't relax, they wouldn't come again. Matthew wanted his classes to be a regular part of every one of his students' schedule. It wasn't about the exercise to Matthew. That was important too, but for Matthew, it was the peace. People just went and went, all day every day. They were too busy to realize they were killing themselves. Matthew wanted to give people a moment to simply be.

Today, for him, there was no peace. He should have been floating on cloud nine. Kit had married him, for fuck's sake. Nothing mattered more. Unfortunately, Kit being his husband had turned Matthew into being twice as possessive. That was way too much jealousy to be married to someone as beautiful as Kit.

In most cases, Matthew would think no one else stood a chance. Kit's gaze rarely wavered from him. Today, Slade O'Neil, a rock star with amazing eyes, chose the mat next to Kit. Slade hadn't stopped flirting or staring since. The longer it went on, the darker Matthew's mood became. He didn't want to end up on the news. That was the only thing stopping Matthew from punching the guy in the throat.

When the class finally ended, Slade lingered for much longer than necessary. It was obvious he wanted Kit alone. The moment it was down to only

Slade, Kit, and Matthew, Slade tossed Matthew an impatient look, as if irritated Matthew wouldn't leave.

Matthew stared back at him, blatantly daring him to say something.

Slade looked away, focused on Kit, and dove in with no care for his life. "What are your plans for the rest of the day?"

Kit shrugged and motioned Matthew's way. "Matthew and I are going to lunch and then I'm joining his flow class."

A sexy smirk touched Slade's lips. Matthew hated him. Fuck, the dude didn't even have one blond hair out of place after thirty minutes of power yoga. "Can I convince you to reschedule those plans and hang out with me instead?"

Kit's smile slipped away.

Matthew's temper did not abate.

Kit motioned toward Matthew again. "Matthew is my husband. I doubt he would appreciate that."

Slade's eyebrows rose. He glanced between them. "Oh. I didn't realize. You weren't wearing a ring and I just assumed..."

Kit waved away Slade's apology. "It's fine. There's no way you could have known."

Slade glanced between them again. He didn't try apologizing to Matthew before focusing on Kit once more. "It was nice meeting you, nonetheless. Maybe I can still sit with you next time."

Kit shrugged. "Sure. I don't see why not."

Slade hung around a bit more, saying his goodbyes. Matthew's temper grew with nowhere to go. It wasn't Kit's fault, but Matthew's anger didn't care. He had too much to lose now, and Matthew was always one wrong move away from completely coming apart.

Unfortunately, the moment they were alone, Matthew's temper found its mark in Kit. "Damn, Kit. I've always loved that you're a flirt, but you think you could let it go in front of me now that we're married."

Kit blinked at the sudden attack. His gaze never wavered from Matthew. Silence dragged on between them. The longer Kit refused to speak, the worse Matthew felt. His guilt didn't cool his temper. In fact, it was like jet fuel on a fire.

"Damn. You can't even deny it. Should I just prepare myself now to be made a fool every day?"

"You remind me of someone."

Matthew's heart dropped. He held his breath.

Kit stared at him a little too hard. Matthew wondered if he would puke.

Kit shook his head, as if shaking off a spell. "It'll come to me." A smile lit Kit's face and Matthew's ire slipped away. In fact, he felt a bit ridiculous as Kit closed the distance between them. He took Matthew's hand. "Come on, baby. Let's snag something to eat from the mall so we can hit the jewelry store. I can't control what other people do, but Slade was right. I'm not wearing a ring, and neither are you. That's unacceptable. I want everyone to know you're mine."

Matthew nearly groaned aloud at his own stupidity. "I love you. You married an ass. I'm so sorry."

Kit never let anything get to him the way anyone else would. He shrugged as they headed for the door. "Maybe I was flirting. This has been my personality for so long that I can't tell anymore. All I can do is try to be better."

Matthew pulled Kit to a stop and hauled him into his arms. For a long moment, he held Kit and said nothing. He kissed Kit's hair. "I'm sorry. There's not a damn thing wrong with you. It was all me."

Kit rubbed his back. "We're fine, baby. Don't worry, okay? We're learning as we go."

They were, but Matthew still felt like he was failing. He loved Kit. It was inevitable Matthew would lose him, but he wasn't ready yet. He needed more time.

*

Kit had never seen Matthew act jealous before. It was kind of hot. The way Matthew had stared down

Slade, obviously ready to fight, made Kit a little too happy. Kit didn't drive people to be possessive. Truthfully, he wasn't much of a prize. While Kit came in a nice package, his attributes were skin deep. Once people got to know him, they didn't find him hot any longer. Matthew was the only exception. He was the only one who mattered. Now, if he could just get Matthew to stop apologizing every five minutes.

"It sucks that your ring has to be sized. I wanted you to have it now."

Matthew squeezed Kit's hand. "I feel like that's one more way I failed you today."

Kit drew a steadying breath through his nose. "Please stop. You have beaten this dead horse all day. If I'm unhappy with you, you'll know it. I'll make sure you're every bit as miserable as I am until you make it right. Seriously, I'll make you sorry for real."

Matthew's smile turned genuine. He brought Kit's hand to his mouth. "One more time. I'm sorry. Now, can I have cuddles? I've been kicking my ass all day and now I need emotional support."

A smile snapped to Kit's lips. He truly loved this man. The first time Matthew had asked him to lunch over a year ago, Kit had only seen Matthew's pretty package. Kit hadn't realized how perfect they would fit. "This plan is acceptable to me, yes."

Matthew held tight to Kit's hand and led him to the bedroom. The bed they shared was king sized, but Kit swore they always only used one side. The other side of the bed was always still perfectly made each morning. They never moved away from holding each other. Once Matthew climbed in, Kit joined him, settling into Matthew's arms.

Time passed without Kit. His entire being stayed focused on Matthew's warmth, touch, and heartbeat. He knew when Matthew finally dozed. A smile tugged at Kit's lips. Matthew didn't snore. He kind of purred. Kit never got enough of every detail of Matthew. Unfortunately, Kit wasn't the least bit tired. He kept hoping that maybe one day he would find a sense of normalcy while he wasn't looking. It hadn't happened yet. Nights never stopped being hard. The fear never went away. Flashbacks held him hostage if he didn't find other ways to distract himself until he passed out.

Kit untangled himself from Matthew's hold. He moved slowly, ensuring Matthew wasn't disturbed. Once Kit was certain Matthew would sleep okay without him, Kit tucked the blanket around him, and sat up. He leaned against the headboard and grabbed his book. The nightlight by the bed was enough for Kit to make out the words. Time slipped away as his gaze slid across the pages, seeing the scenes play out inside his mind.

Matthew whimpered.

Kit's gaze moved to his face. It was screwed up in pain. As Kit looked on, sweat beaded Matthew's skin. Kit set his book aside and brushed his fingers through Matthew's hair.

Matthew's eyes shot open. They looked dead. Kit could tell he was still asleep. He had that sleep-walking look about him—like he wasn't there.

Kit kept his voice soft. "Are you okay?"

Matthew's dead eyes focused on Kit. "He's coming."

Kit's chest tightened. Chill bumps raced down

his skin. Fear sideswiped him.

Matthew whimpered again.

Kit tried harder to break the spell that kept Matthew trapped. "It's okay, baby. I've got you."

Tears welled in Matthew's eyes. "I can't keep you safe." Before Kit could react, Matthew's body bowed. He started swinging, fighting an invisible foe. Matthew was wild with fear. His cries tore at Kit's heart. Kit turned desperate in his attempt to pull Matthew from his nightmare. He shook Matthew and called his name. Nothing broke through his terror. A solid elbow connected with Kit's nose. Blood splashed the sheets as Kit cried out in pain.

Matthew leapt from the bed. His crazed gaze scanned the room before settling on Kit. Blood gushed from Kit. He tried staunching the flow without luck.

"Oh my god, Kit. Are you okay?"

Kit tried nodding. Between the pain, the blood, and his fear, he wasn't sure if he succeeded.

Matthew rushed to his side and plucked him from the bed. After rushing him inside the bathroom, Matthew set Kit on the vanity. He grabbed a washcloth and wet it with warm water before trying to clean away the blood.

Kit couldn't look away from Matthew's face. Tears streamed down his cheeks. Kit wondered if Matthew even noticed. Not for the first time, Kit questioned if he knew Matthew at all. They always avoided talking about the past. Kit had nothing good to say. He worried if he asked Matthew about his past, then Matthew would want to trade. Kit couldn't go there. Judging by Matthew's scars and his story about Kit saving him from suicide by cop, Kit imagined Matthew didn't want to go there either. Now he wondered if not talking had been a mistake. He felt like he was staring at a stranger.

Matthew kept apologizing.

The shock finally dissipated enough for Kit to speak. "Stop. You were having a nightmare. I know you'd never hit me on purpose."

More tears streamed down Matthew's cheeks. His face screwed up in pain. "That's no excuse."

Matthew felt unreachable in that moment. Kit felt helpless. He didn't know how to fix what he didn't understand.

After checking behind the washcloth, Matthew seemed satisfied Kit had stopped bleeding. He tossed the cloth in the sink. He gripped the edge of the counter. His knuckles turned white as he stared at the bathroom floor. Kit stared at the top of Matthew's bowed head, waiting for the explosion. He swore he felt the pressure building in the bathroom, getting ready to level everything in its path.

Matthew finally straightened. "Don't move. I'll grab you a clean shirt."

Kit's mouth opened. He didn't know what he planned to say. Matthew disappeared before he could say a thing.

He returned a few seconds later, empty-handed. "I can't think. Let's just get you out of these bloody clothes. You usually sleep nude anyhow."

With a nod, Kit let Matthew gently undress him. This seemed important. He could feel Matthew's need to care for him. Once he was nude, Matthew carried Kit back to bed and tucked him in.

Kit felt like a black hole had opened in his chest. Despite Matthew's loving touch, Matthew looked like he had mentally retreated. Kit could feel Matthew withdrawing from him a little more by the second.

Matthew whisked his lips across Kit's. "Get some sleep, angel. I love you."

Panic shot through Kit. "I love you too. Aren't you joining me?"

With a shake of his head, Matthew never met his gaze. "I just need a minute, okay? I'll be back before you can miss me."

Kit already missed him. Something didn't feel right. Kit didn't know how to fix it. His face throbbed and Matthew looked ready to bolt. Nothing felt right anymore. He was terrified, and Kit wondered if he would be sick. But, for whatever reason, Kit simply agreed and watched as Matthew left him alone.

For several minutes, Kit stared at the ceiling. The pressure in his chest wouldn't ease. He swore shadows moved through the room, transporting Kit back to the days of helplessness. He fought a wave of tears. Kit couldn't stand this feeling. The knot in his stomach was as familiar as breathing. Kit couldn't take it. He slipped from the bed, half expecting a monster from the past to pull him back down onto the mattress. That horrible sensation never faltered as Kit tiptoed from the bedroom. Some nightmares never ended. Once his past caught him in its grasp, Kit always had a hard time shaking it. Maybe he should make Matthew and him a pot of coffee. They could stay awake all night and slay the demons together. The more Kit thought about it, the more he liked the idea.

Kit headed for the kitchen first. He started the coffee before going in search of Matthew. Getting accidentally punched was nothing. Matthew had no idea how well Kit could take a hit. Matthew's office door was closed. Kit turned the knob, half expecting to find it locked. He was more than a little surprised when the knob easily turned beneath his hand. The room was dark except for the open bathroom doorway inside Matthew's office. Kit couldn't explain his sudden fear, but the place felt devoid of life. He found his feet moving faster the closer he got to the bathroom. It was empty, but a bloody razor blade rested on the vanity.

Kit turned in a circle, hunting for any hint of where Matthew had gone. He ran back into the office and turned on the lights. There was no sign of him. A folded piece of paper sat on Matthew's desk. Kit snatched up the paper as he caught sight of his name.

Kit,

You can't help me.

I love you,

Matt

What the fuck? Kit raced through the entire house. He searched every room. Matthew was nowhere to be found. Finally, he headed for the garage. Matthew's Audi was gone. Kit's shoulders fell. His knees nearly collapsed. Matthew was out there somewhere, bleeding and alone. Kit had no idea where to start looking. He was helpless all over again.

Chapter Seven

On day three of no word from Matthew, something inside Kit snapped. He had already called all the hospitals with no luck. Even as Matthew's husband, privacy laws stopped him from learning a thing. He had left a note, so the general consensus was that Matthew had abandoned him. Kit had nothing but his inner panic to keep him company. But on day three, the anger set in.

Kit wasn't sleeping. His rage had nowhere to go. Some sort of fuck Matthew took over Kit. He packed his things. If Matthew could run away, leaving Kit a mess, so could Kit. He almost made it out the door when he remembered his birth certificate. He couldn't leave anything behind. Kit never, ever wanted to set eyes on this house again.

He had reinvented himself once before. Kit would do it again. This time, he wouldn't let another soul touch his heart or body. Matthew had shown Kit had zero sense.

He quickly typed the number Matthew had shown him into the safe. He grabbed the stack of papers Matthew had put inside. As he moved to pull the pages from the safe, a file underneath caught his eye. It was a yellow folder with an attorney's emblem printed on the front. Kit might not have noticed anything about the file folder if his name wasn't written on top.

Kit set the paperwork aside and reached for the folder. His hand shook as he pulled it from the safe. An overwhelming feeling of dread washed over him as he flipped open the folder. There was a picture of him inside. He remembered the image. Kit had taken it with his phone just after he turned twelve. He had borrowed his mom's makeup and painted his face. At the time, he had thought he looked so adorable. It had been his secret. His mom had found the image, and a huge fight had exploded between them. It had dragged on for days until Kit had stormed off during their fight. That was where his nightmare had begun. He didn't understand why the picture was in Matthew's safe.

Kit flipped the photo over and inspected the next page. His knees gave out. Kit found himself sitting in Matthew's office chair. His hands shook so badly, he could barely hang on to the file. There was a letter from Kit's mom, begging Thomas Ricci—the man who had held Kit against his will for three years—for help with her son. She lamented the fact that her son seemed to be turning gay. It seemed they had spoken on Facebook in a group for parents with difficult children.

Sweat broke out on Kit's upper lip and forehead. He brushed it away and turned to the next page. Once again, there was a letter from his mom. It consisted of four words. *Take him. He's yours.*

Tears slipped down Kit's cheeks. He turned the page. It was a coroner's report, ruling Thomas' death a suicide. The next page had an image of Kit two years ago. He was at the mall, looking at his phone while he walked. A report was attached, listing all known addresses and possible numbers. It looked exactly like a dossier from a private investigation. Kit flipped back to the beginning and found a business card tucked into a slot inside the folder's front cover. He eyed the name: Lance Hughes, Private Investigator. He had an L.A.

address. Kit quickly dug out his phone and searched the address. It was only fifteen minutes away. He closed the file and tucked it beneath his arm. Someone was about to tell him what in the fuck was going on or he would commit a second murder. Kit had already gotten away with it once. Thankfully, his anger and confusion stopped his hands shaking by the time he reached his destination. In the parking lot of Gaines and Stanley law offices, Kit applied a light coating of makeup and prepared for battle.

He shoved the file and his gun into an oversized bag and headed for the door. At this point, there was no going back and no low too low for Kit. He had already decided he would storm the place if they forced his hand. Kit opened the door and stepped right into a solid wall of man. He was easily six foot and dark-haired. His green eyes might have mesmerized Kit, if Kit hadn't been such a mess. He reached out to steady Kit when Kit nearly bounced off his solid muscle. Kit jumped away before the guy could grab him. There was no way Kit could handle being touched right now. As their gazes collided, Kit saw the guy's recognition and shock. He tried rearranging his features, but it was too late.

"Lance Hughes?"

The guy's eyes shot from side to side, as if looking for an escape.

Kit wasn't having it. "There's no sense in making a run for it."

"Um."

Kit didn't have time for this shit. "There's a gun in my bag. I will shoot you dead in this parking lot if you don't get in my SUV right now."

Lance's eyebrows raised. A hint of humor touched his features. "No wonder Matthew can't resist you."

Kit didn't smile. His life had been turned upside down and there was no happiness anymore. He would not live his life in fear and doubt. Lance would explain this file or Kit would kill him.

Lance's smile disappeared. "Which SUV?"

It was Kit's turn to raise his eyebrows. "You put together a pretty extensive file on me. Don't you know?"

To his surprise, Lance's chest expanded on a deep breath, as if bracing himself for anything. "Yeah." He headed for Kit's Navigator.

Kit hit the button on his keys, unlocking the doors. He kept one eye locked on Lance and one hand locked on the gun in his bag. Kit was too far gone to fuck around anymore. Lance climbed into the passenger seat and closed the door. Kit locked the doors as he climbed behind the wheel.

"I'm not trying to piss you off or anything, but you do know I can just hit the button and unlock the door, right?"

Kit flashed him a smile that felt evil even to him. "Not in this vehicle."

Lance tried. Nothing happened.

Kit's wicked smiled turned malicious, even though he didn't bother showing it to Lance. Instead, he pulled the file from his bag. "Start talking. Why was this in my husband's safe?"

Lance didn't reach for the folder. "Matthew hired me a few years back to find you."

That answered exactly nothing. "How did he get this old picture of me and why does he have letters from my mom?"

For a moment, Lance stared at him in silence. Finally, his chest expanded on a deep breath again. "Matthew's grandfather was Thomas Ricci. The pictures and letters were his."

Everything inside Kit went cold. He couldn't breathe. Everything hurt. Kit didn't know if a person could die from feeling too much at once, but he thought he might find out if the shocks kept coming. He couldn't decide what to ask next. Kit knew there must be questions he should ask. Nothing left his lips. His brain had frozen.

Lance took pity on him. "Matthew's parents were killed in a car accident when he was four." Lance did air quotes around accident, letting him know the likelihood was slim that it was true. "Thomas took custody of Matthew immediately. No one balked. Thomas was Matthew's grandfather. He was rich, powerful, and a decorated war hero. Not a single soul questioned a thing." Lance visibly swallowed, as if he didn't want to continue, but he did. "Thomas began grooming him right away."

Kit's eyes fell closed. Twelve had been a nightmare age for Kit, but four? His poor baby.

Lance didn't take pity on him and stop. "He started losing interest in Matthew around sixteen. He had gotten too old for Thomas' tastes. Over the years, Matthew had watched several young boys come into the home in short bursts, only to mysteriously disappear. I've come to believe they were either passed along to someone else in his circles or killed. Either way, Matthew was the only boy spared the same fate because he was blood. Still, he lived in constant fear. He was seriously messed up, as you can imagine. But then Thomas got his sights set on you. I don't know what you did. I don't want to know. Whatever it was, I'm sure it was what it took to survive, but you caught and held his attention. So much so, Thomas set up a new home for you in Texas and stayed."

Kit knew that much. No one needed to recant his story. He relived it all the time in his nightmares.

"Matthew sees you as the person who saved him. He also sees you as his biggest failure. After Thomas died, everything he possessed came to Matthew. He changed his name from Matthieu Ricci to Matthew Ross and hired me to be in charge of the search to find you. Matthew saw his silence as equal to Thomas's crime. He tried killing himself with alcohol and drugs, razor blades, and he even shot himself once."

"Then he saw me in a magazine," Kit finished for him.

Lance's eyebrows rose, showing his surprise, but he nodded. "Yeah. Once he knew you were alive, he became a man obsessed. He did everything he could to get clean. I've never seen anyone work harder at turning their life around." A small smile touched Lance's lips. His gaze moved over Kit's face. "I don't think he intended to ever meet you. He just wanted to know you were okay. Matthew couldn't stomach the idea of you ending up like him. Then you walked through the door of Fitness Titan and swept him away. He says you're the strongest person he's ever met. That you're a firecracker. I see now why he thinks that."

Pain had Kit in a chokehold. His baby had suffered and stayed silent. He was out there somewhere, and Kit was fucking helpless. Kit swallowed past the pain. "Do you know where he is?"

Lance blew out a breath.

Kit almost begged.

Thankfully, Lance spilled before Kit lost his pride. "After he hit you the other night, he came a bit unglued. He cut himself, which he hasn't done in at least two years. Lying to you and keeping secrets has been silently undermining all his hard work. He checked himself in to Wilderness Garden Mental Health Clinic."

Kit gave a sharp nod. He didn't know if it was for Lance or himself. "Okay. Good." He didn't feel better, but he didn't feel worse either. "Knowledge is power, and I have answers. I can deal with that." He unlocked the door. "I appreciate your time."

Lance didn't budge. His gaze never wavered from Kit. "Are you okay?"

Kit stared at nothing with no answer. He wasn't sure if he had ever been okay, but he would survive. Kit always did.

"Why don't you let me drive you home? You look a little pale."

Kit shot him an irritated look. "You can go fuck yourself with that bullshit. I've never looked bad a day in my whole goddamn life."

Lance made a calming gesture. "I just meant that you've had a trying day."

With a snort, Kit looked away. "This doesn't even rate in my top one hundred of bad days."

"I imagine that's true." Lance fell silent, but he still didn't leave Kit alone.

Kit found his gaze sliding back Lance's way.

Lance silently watched him. His eyes looked haunted—like he had seen too much. Kit found himself saying more than he should. "Your investigative skills could use some polish."

Lance looked as if he fought a laugh. "Is that so? What did I miss?"

Kit reached over and popped open the glovebox. He pulled out an envelope and handed it to Lance. As Lance unfolded the papers, Kit explained the contents. "After I watched Thomas die, I burned everything he had given me, and opened his laptop to his child porn. I left it all for the police to see. His politician friends covered it all up, of course. But on my way out, I unlocked his safe and found that receipt along with my birth certificate and social security card. My mom didn't give me away in hopes of saving me from the gay.

She sold me for twenty grand—like a car." Lance's gaze lifted from the damning proof Kit carried with him everywhere and latched on to Kit. Kit refused to look weak. "So I took eighty grand as my payment. The world is better for his death."

Lance nodded and looked away. "Unfortunately, there are countless others just like him."

That was true, but Kit couldn't kill them all.

Kit drew an unsteady breath. "Will you do me a favor?"

Lance didn't hesitate. "Sure."

"I know Matthew doesn't want to talk to me since I'm making him sick or whatever, but if you do speak with him, will you pass along a message?"

"Yeah. Anything."

Kit took another breath for courage. "Let him

know that I'll be around. If he wants a divorce, then I understand. I just want him healthy."

Lance's shoulders fell. He looked completely defeated. "Yeah. If I hear from him, I'll let him know."

Kit nodded, even though he died a little at the idea of Matthew divorcing him. His whole life, all Kit wanted was exactly what Matthew gave him. Life was way too fucked up for Kit to quit on the one person who actually loved him. A wave of exhaustion and heartache washed over Kit. Of course his love would be killing Matthew. That was what Kit did. He watched things die. His eyes fell closed. He should have shared Thomas's final meal. There was nothing for him in this world.

*

It felt like it took forever for Matthew to regain his

phone privileges. Unfortunately, a few days after checking himself into this nightmare situation, Matthew had awoken from a dead and medicated sleep to perfect clarity. He had forgotten to remove that folder from his safe. If Kit left, and he didn't doubt for a second Kit would leave, he would find that file. He had been a mess until he could finally call Lance.

Thankfully, Lance answered on the third ring, putting Matthew out of his misery.

"I need you to do one last job for me," Matthew said without waiting for a greeting.

Lance didn't hesitate. "Of course. Anything."

"Go to my place and destroy the file on Kit." Matthew didn't know if Kit had checked the safe or if Kit was still at home waiting, but Matthew had to try one more time to reclaim his fake life. That wouldn't happen if Kit learned the truth.

Lance cleared his throat. "Um, I can't do that."

Matthew wondered if he would break down again. "Why?"

Another uncomfortable-sounding throat-clearing came through the line. "Kit's already been to see me. He's already read the file."

A wave of pain had Matthew squeezing his eyes closed. "How much does he know?"

"Everything."

Matthew took a few breaths, trying to make his lungs work properly. "Damn. Is he okay?"

Lance blew out a breath that sounded loud in Matthew's ear. "I don't know. He's kind of a tough cookie to get a read on, but he did ask me to tell you something if we spoke."

Matthew squeezed the phone a little tighter.

"And?"

"He said if you want a divorce, he understands."

Matthew tugged at his hair. "I don't want a divorce. Why in the fuck would I want that?"

Lance snorted. "Maybe it has a little to do with you running out on him. I mean, how did you expect him to take that?" Lance immediately backpedaled. "Ignore that. You're working on yourself and that's exactly what you should be doing. I don't know why I said that."

"Because it's true," Matthew said, hearing the defeat in his own voice. He pressed his forehead against the wall. "Did he look okay?"

"He looked a little pale, but when I mentioned it, he told me to go fuck myself."

Matthew smiled. "He's a bit explosive."

Lance chuckled. "He is that. Just work on getting better, Matt. I slapped a GPS tracker on his SUV. He won't get away again."

A laugh caught in Matthew's throat. "Thanks for that."

"Don't worry. I'll bill you for it."

He shook his head. Matthew didn't doubt it. "He's worth every penny. I need him to be safe."

Lance made a sound of approval. "I've got my eye on him. Everything will hold until you get home."

Matthew took a calming breath. It wasn't like he had any other choice but to wait. If there was any chance at all that Kit didn't hate him, Matthew had to come out of this whole. Kit deserved a steady man. If Kit hated him, then Kit deserved to know Matthew lived a long, healthy, and miserable life as punishment. That was the right thing to do.

Chapter Eight

Every day dragged into the next. Kit kept breathing.

It wasn't like him to sit still, so he didn't. Kit took

over teaching Matthew's yoga classes so he would

still have a job when he was ready. He knew

Matthew didn't need the money, but they needed the

peace his classes brought. Lance had taken up

coming to Kit's classes and having coffee with Kit

twice a week. He took on a few modeling gigs and

did a bit role. Whatever it took to keep him getting

out of bed, Kit did it. Lance said Matthew didn't

want a divorce. Kit clung hard to that knowledge.

He would be damned if he let Thomas steal another

damn thing from him from beyond the grave. If Kit

lost Matthew, then Thomas had beaten them both.

Kit had even stopped trading in his books.

Instead, he filled an empty room with shelves and kept each novel he read. Each time he added a book to one of the shelves, he felt like he put down another root. Kit refused to think of this place as the house where Thomas Ricci's grandson lived. Instead, he decided to shape it into the home he shared with his husband. That was how it would stay until Matthew decided if he could handle loving Kit.

Despite his best efforts, Kit still didn't like being alone. He spent more time by the pool reading than he did indoors. There were ghosts in Kit's head.

A shadow fell over Kit's book. Kit didn't bother swallowing his irritation over the interruption. Their neighbors were the worst. "For fuck's sake, Cindy. This is why nobody likes you."

"Actually, nobody likes Cindy because she jumps on every sale from home scheme that comes along. She constantly posts all her stupid invitations on the community Facebook page alongside her constant admonishments for breaking HOA rules."

Kit's head shot up at the sound of Matthew's voice. He couldn't believe his eyes. "Hey."

Matthew looked good. He looked beautiful, even while shifting from foot to foot. "Hey."

Kit didn't know how to act. There was nothing to say. He fought the urge to ask if he should leave. "Why didn't you tell me you were coming home?"

Matthew looked uncomfortable as hell. "I wasn't sure you would still be here."

"Why?"

Matthew didn't bother pretending. "Because of your chat with Lance."

"Why does that matter?" Kit couldn't stop. He needed answers and he didn't know where to start.

"He said he told you everything."

It was hard. There were so many paths Kit could choose, but really, he had already chosen the day he killed Thomas. He had picked survival. Kit had chosen to no longer be Thomas' victim. He needed Matthew to pick that path too.

Kit moved his feet, making room for Matthew. "Sit."

Matthew sat. His gaze never wavered from Kit.

Kit didn't hold back. Staring at Matthew reaffirmed every decision Kit had made in the past four months. "Look, baby. When I moved to California, I made freedom into my whole personality. Maybe I didn't want anyone touching me again, but that's because I needed to heal. I'll never be angry with you, if you need extra help to heal too." Kit waved away part of his statement. "Unless you don't tell me again. That was crappy, but I will never hold asking for help against you."

Matthew didn't look less uncomfortable. "I told so many lies. You deserved to know where I came from."

The backs of Kit's eyes stung at Matthew's broken tone. Kit couldn't let Matthew hurt. He refused to let Matthew think Kit could ever love him less. "We don't get to pick our families."

Matthew visibly swallowed. "Please don't make excuses for me. I may be a mess, but I can take it. Tell me you hate me, and you hate that I carry his blood. Don't pretend this is okay."

Kit punched him in the arm. "Shut up, if you only plan to be stupid. I love you. You are the one for me. That hasn't changed. If you can't get onboard with that, you should have accepted my divorce offer months ago. You didn't. So guess what? You're fucking stuck with me. What do you plan to do about it?"

Matthew's gorgeous smile was everything Kit hoped for. "I lost my shit a little over hurting you."

Kit nodded. "Ya think?"

Matthew's smile slipped away. "I can't promise I won't flip out again."

While holding Matthew's stare, Kit scooted closer. He took Matthew's hand. Kit swore electricity shot up his arm at the contact. He had never craved anyone's touch until Matthew. Now he couldn't stop. "I love you."

Matthew's grip tightened on Kit's hand. "I love you too."

A lump rose in Kit's throat. "Don't leave again without an explanation. If you're hurting, say it. If you need more help than I can give, I'll drive you. I was so scared when I couldn't find you."

Matthew nodded. He shifted positions and crawled into the lounge chair next to Kit. Their lips brushed as Kit settled into Matthew's arms. Kit fought the way his heart tried beating a little too fast.

Matthew, proving he was the perfect match for Kit, acted as if the past four months hadn't happened. He picked up Kit's book and held it in one hand while Kit kept his other arm occupied. "So you thought I was Cindy, huh? Has she been that bad?"

Kit stroked Matthew's stomach. He hated confrontation more than almost anything. It always made him feel sick and took him back to the days of being Thomas's toy. Kit needed the peace Matthew offered. "The worst. I think she has a crush on you and is totally convinced I buried your body in the basement."

Matthew kissed Kit's temple. "We don't have a basement."

"Yeah. That's what I told her. She sent us a violation letter for the Pride flag. So I've been sunbathing in the nude. I know she's spying, but the only way she can say anything about my lewd behavior is if she admits to it."

"A standoff. I love it. Maybe we should move into a more accepting neighborhood, though? We have enough going on in our lives without fighting her."

Kit gasped. "Hush your mouth. This is our

newlywed home. I thrive on drama. Bring it, Cindy."

Matthew fell silent and Kit panicked. He could feel Matthew turn brooding. He turned up the cheerfulness to counterbalance the moment. "You know what I should do? I should run for HOA president. Is that a thing? Running, I mean. I should do that."

Matthew trailed his fingertips down Kit's arm. "He never lived here."

Kit's throat swelled. He knew they couldn't avoid this forever. "I don't care." Kit shrugged. "Maybe I should, but I don't feel him here. You know I don't like to be alone. I can't sleep. That's not true here. It's home. I only feel us when I'm here. Nothing else matters. I know in my heart that if you found those letters before Thomas' death, you would've saved me. You don't have to think about that aspect of things again. I completely believe in you."

Matthew's hold tightened on Kit. "I don't deserve you. I'm so sorry for everything."

Kit rubbed Matthew's stomach. "You're home now. I don't care about anything else. FYI, though. If you ever leave me again without telling me what's up, we're never having sex again. You know I can do it too. I went seven years without it, with no problem before you. I have no problem flying in the face of convention and keeping this booty to myself."

Matthew set Kit's book aside and linked fingers with Kit. "You're my heart. I'd stay with you sex or no sex, but I can't put myself through that again either. I just want to be whole for you."

Kit snuggled as close as he could get. He had missed this more than words. Just holding Matthew meant more to Kit than anything. "I'm not worried. We're pretty fucking spectacular together. I believe in us."

"Damn. I really missed holding you."

The emotion in Matthew's voice had Kit holding him tighter. He didn't doubt Matthew had expected to come home to a mess. Fortunately, Kit had plenty of time to think over the last four months. He had turned things over in his mind, looking at every possible angle. Everything always came down to the foundation. He loved Matthew, and Matthew was a good man. Matthew had treated Kit like a king since the day they met. Kit had watched Matthew be the opposite of everything his grandfather had been. Life had been very cruel to them, but Kit had to admit it had been much crueler to Matthew. Matthew didn't deserve Kit's hatred or fury. He didn't deserve to be punished for the crimes committed against him. They were better than what had been done to them. Kit wanted to leave the past where it belonged.

Kit snuggled as close as he could get. He nuzzled Matthew's chest and inhaled his scent. They could and would be happy. Kit was extremely good at forcing life to go his way. This would be no different. Matthew belonged to him. Kit would love him and keep him safe as long as they both lived, as he had vowed to do. There was nowhere he would rather be.

*

They didn't move for hours. Matthew's mind was quiet for the first time in a long time. He read Kit's book aloud to him while they soaked up each other's touch. Matthew didn't get a lot of internal peace, but Kit always gave it to him. Lying to Kit had been undermining every bit of progress he had made over the years. That was over now. If Kit still loved him after learning the truth, Matthew could face anything. Right here, in his lounge chair by the pool, Matthew held the world. He was complete.

Unfortunately, he was still adjusting to the combo of anti-depressants and anxiety meds they had found worked the best for him. He still got tired faster than he liked. Matthew found it harder to focus on the words with each passing moment. His eyelids grew heavy.

Kit took the book from his hand. "Come on, sleepy baby. Let's go take a shower and cuddle in bed. I'll hold you while you sleep."

A grateful smile tugged at Matthew's lips. He never wanted to stop holding Kit. Inside their bathroom, Kit slowly undressed Matthew before stripping away his clothes. Matthew's sleepy haze disappeared, and his body stirred as Kit's beautiful nude form stole every ounce of his attention. He felt like the luckiest man on the planet. Matthew had come home expecting the worst. Instead, he had been greeted with perfect peace and flawless love. Kit definitely possessed a quiet grace he didn't get enough credit for having. He could be so explosive that those moments were the ones that stood out in people's minds when they pictured Kit. Matthew never took for granted this version of Kit. He stood steady and loyal with the people he loved. Matthew hadn't truly believed he would fall in that category. He wouldn't doubt Kit again.

Kit took his time, babying Matthew in the shower. He gently washed Matthew's hair and stole kisses every few seconds. Matthew ate up every ounce of attention. When Kit kissed his cheek, Matthew stole his chance. He turned his head and claimed Kit's mouth. Their tongues brushed. Matthew's heart sighed. He was sickeningly in love with Kit. He dreamed about Kit all the time. There was no one else for him.

"I love you," Matthew said against Kit's lips as he killed the water in the shower. "I need to take you to bed."

Matthew grabbed a thick towel and dried Kit's body. He took his time, ensuring Kit was every bit as aroused as him before carrying him to bed. They kissed and touched for what felt like hours. Matthew found himself linking his fingers through

Kit's and holding tight as his body moved against Kit's. Kit's kiss turned hotter by the second. A moan vibrated around their tongues. Matthew worked to pull another from Kit. Kit tore his mouth away, gasping and straining. The sight punched Matthew in the gut. He couldn't look away. Kit was always beyond beautiful. On the edge of orgasm, he was the definition of perfection. He couldn't believe Kit stayed. Matthew was more than moved. He was blown away. Matthew knew he didn't deserve Kit, but Kit made him believe that he could.

Matthew's arousal couldn't be ignored. His body burned. The friction between them had Matthew ready to blow. He couldn't hold back. Thankfully, at the last second before Matthew exploded, Kit cried out. His entire body jerked in Matthew's arms. Even through his soul-rocking ecstasy, Matthew never closed his eyes against the sight of Kit's passion. He held the entire fucking world in this bed. Matthew would keep him safe for the rest of their lives. He would never leave him again. Matthew might be thick sometimes, but he always learned from his mistakes. Kit was his past, present, and future. Matthew would never question their solidarity again.

*

Until the moment Matthew took Kit inside, Lance watched their entire exchange. He sat in his truck, transfixed as Matthew read from the book he held and Kit hung on his every word. They were a beautiful couple. It was restorative to Lance's soul to see something so amazing bloom from something beyond ugly. They gave him hope. A smile tugged at Lance's lips without thought. Kit had fire. He was exactly what Matthew needed to stay on track. Each time Lance thought about how Kit had threatened his life, he swallowed back a laugh. Kit had absolutely meant it. He would kill for Matthew. Still, Kit was one of a kind. Lance liked him a lot.

A banging on his window had Lance's heart leaping into his throat. A middle-aged woman with short platinum hair waited for Lance to roll down his window. He knew immediately the woman had "Live, Laugh, Love" stenciled on at least one wall inside her house, but she didn't live by any of those standards. Lance mentally braced himself for whatever hell she came bearing.

"I called the police."

Lance fought an eye roll. He flipped open his wallet and flashed her a badge. "I am the police."

She barely spared the badge a glance. Her gaze

moved toward Kit and Matthew's house. "Is there something illegal happening here?" She looked like she relished the idea of Kit and Matthew doing something wrong.

Lance gave her a sharp nod. "Yes, ma'am. We've received several complaints of a middle-aged blonde woman harassing the residents of this property. We're investigating this as a hate crime. I've been keeping an eye on the place, but you're the only person I've seen so far. You wouldn't know anything about that, would you?"

Her expression had Lance fighting hard to keep his expression blank. "I live next door. I'll keep an eye out."

"You do that." Lance bit the inside of his cheek as he rolled up his window. He needed to get out of here before the police showed up, but he hoped he had helped Kit with his neighbor issues. That was the least Lance could do to help two people who had been failed by the rest of the world. He knew they would be okay as long as they had each other. Still, Lance would hang around in their lives just to be safe. They needed someone on their side.

Chapter Nine

Kit sat on his yoga mat at the front of the class and watched Matthew expose his heart. He was honest and raw as he explained how living with severe depression had led to his extended absence. Matthew thanked his students for sticking through his long hiatus. Kit was proud as hell to be married to such an amazing man.

Lance sat at Kit's side, being the surprisingly supportive friend Kit never expected, but needed. Zep and Frost had welcomed preemie twins a week before Matthew had come home. All of his friends had lives. No one had been free to hold his hand the way he did for everyone else. While Kit knew he wasn't particularly lovable, he tried his damnedest for everyone in his life. He didn't expect anyone's life to stop for him. Kit was used to being alone. But the last four months of his life had been a trial, and he needed someone to force their friendship on him. Lance had been that guy.

Everyone stood as Matthew called an end to the class. Several people bombarded Matthew to wish him well or share stories. Kit turned Lance's way and was nearly mowed down by Slade instead.

"Hey, Kit. How have you been? I didn't know about any of this. I've been on tour. I see you got a wedding ring." He dropped his sunglasses.

Lance bent down to get them.

So did Slade.

Their heads collided.

"Ow. Goddamn." Lance came up with the sunglasses and rubbing his head.

"Shit. I'm sorry." Slade reached for the glasses

and somehow poked Lance in the eye.

Lance smacked his hand over the offended eye. "Holy shit."

Slade winced. "Fuck. My bad."

Kit bit his bottom lip, trying not to laugh.

Slade pried his sunglasses from Lance's hand. "I'll just take these."

Lance glared at Slade. His eye was red as hell.

Kit tried smoothing things over. "Hey, Slade. This is Lance. Lance, meet Slade."

Lance was slow to shake hands—like he worried what damage Slade would do next.

"Did you say you've been on tour?"

Slade nodded. "Yeah. Worldwide. Our final stop was in Australia. That's why I'm such a tragedy today. Sorry again. Like, I don't even know what day it is."

"It's Thursday."

Slade laughed. "Dude. I thought it was Friday."

Lance shook his head. The irritation in expression had melted away. Now he couldn't seem to take his eyes off Slade. Kit took the opportunity to slip away while they were distracted. Matthew waited for him. He seemed to light up from the inside as Kit headed his way. Kit swore his eyes got brighter. There were some things people couldn't fake. Matthew loved Kit. Kit couldn't get enough.

"How are you feeling after your first class back?"

"Like I'm ready for another."

Kit wrapped his arms around Matthew's waist and settled into Matthew's embrace. "I guess it's a good thing you have more scheduled then."

Matthew kissed Kit's cheek. "Not for another

hour or so. We should close the door and spend some time alone."

"But we're not..." Kit turned to find the room empty. He blinked at the sight. "Wow. Where did everyone go?"

"They cleared out the second you touched me." He kissed Kit's ear. "I guess we look desperate for each other."

A soft chuckle escaped Kit. His eyes fell closed as Matthew kissed his ear again. "I don't doubt it. I'm always desperate for you." Kit forced himself to focus. "Also, I'm super proud of you. The way you spoke today took a lot of courage. You had everyone teary-eyed and engrossed."

Matthew pulled away, looking nervous. He moved to close the door. "Um. I'm glad you feel that way, because I've been wanting to talk to you about something."

Kit nodded. He could see whatever it was, it was important to Matthew. "Okay. We've got time."

Matthew drew an audible breath. "Okay, so, while I was in the hospital, Lance put me in touch with this guy named Zander. He owns a bunch of hotels and casinos here on the west coast. It turns out that Zander is also a survivor of human trafficking and he plans to start an advocacy thing. For personal reasons, he can't be the face of this project. He's only wanting to finance the startup. I didn't drop your name, but I told him that my husband and I were both survivors and that you're an actor. Even though we don't need the money and you might not want to be the face of this thing with me, I thought I would throw it out there so we can talk about it."

Kit could see the hope in Matthew's eyes. He needed this. Maybe Kit did too. Kit slowly nodded, running everything through his mind. "Well, you know me. I refuse to be ashamed. Staying silent means Thomas wins. It means my mom gets to live her life like I never existed. I think we should meet with this guy and see what he has to say."

Matthew visibly tried not to hope. "Okay. I mean, it can't hurt to talk, right? If we can't do what he needs, then at least we'll know we took the offer seriously."

"Exactly." Kit loved how excited and proud Matthew looked. There was nothing he wouldn't do to keep Matthew feeling strong.

Matthew closed the distance between them. "I'll get it set up." His hands slid across Kit's hips. "In the meantime, I still feel like I have four months of snuggles and kisses to make up. Should we lock the door?"

Happiness welled inside Kit. "We should definitely lock the door." Kit didn't know where this advocate thing would go, but they had their entire lives to figure it out. Right now, Kit had a sexy and amazing husband to kiss and snuggle. Matthew was right. They had four months of lost time to make up. While Matthew needed the relaxation that his classes brought, they had plenty of time in between to squeeze in some loving. Kit could definitely see himself spending the rest of his life just like this. This was the good type of forever. Kit couldn't wait to get started.

*

The International Labour Organization estimates that 1.2 million children are trafficked each year. A few of my books have touched on this subject over the years because this is an enormous problem that doesn't get nearly the coverage it deserves. There is an organization called Thorn that builds technology to defend children from sex trafficking. Times are really tough all around the world right now, but if you have the ability to give, Thorn accepts donations of any amount here: https://www.thorn.org/donate/ Always be a force for good in any way that you can and thank you for reading.

Keep an eye out for the next Candied Crush, *Beautifully Wicked.*

Please consider leaving a review at the retailer where you purchased this book. Reviews really help with a book's visibility, which allows me to continue writing more stories. Thank you, Charity.

About the Author

Charity Parkerson is an award-winning and multi-published author with several companies. Born with no filter from her brain to her mouth, she decided to take this odd quirk and insert it in her characters.

*Eight-time Readers' Favorite Award Winner
*2015 Passionate Plume Award Finalist
*2013 Reviewers' Choice Award Winner
*2012 ARRA Finalist for Favorite Paranormal Romance
*Five-time winner of The Mistress of the Darkpath

Connect with her online:

—Sign up for my newsletter: https://sendfox.com/charityparkerson
http://bit.ly/CharityNews
—Join my readers' group on Facebook: http://bit.ly/CharitysTribe
—Website: charityparkerson.com — Facebook: facebook.com/authorCharityParkersonfacebook.com/TheMenofSin—Twitter: twitter.com/CharityParkerso

—Instagram:
Instagram.com/sinnerauthor
—Bookbub:
https://www.bookbub.com/authors/charity-parkerson
—Amazon page:
author.to/CharityParkerson
(http://author.to/CharityParkerson)